Underworld

Ivy Cole

Book Cover by Bookbrush

Image for cover by Photo by Keith Pottinger : https://www.pexels.com/photo/woman-in-black-clothes-posing-on-throne-17980369/

Edited by Kyla Lee

Heading Illustrations by pikisuperstar on Freepik

Cover page photo Photo by Burak Evlivan

Trigger Warning:

This book contains mentions of blood, abuse, and guns. PTSD of torture, abuse, and mentions of rape. This is your warning; please be advised. This book does contain MM.

Hades Dedication:

To all my masculine peeps out there. This dedication is for you. The legend of Hades depends on the story you are reading. Our Hades is a protector and defends those who are weaker. So embrace your inner Hades. Protect those who need protection. Defend those who need defending. Stand by your beliefs, but don't be a twat waffle about it. And those who wish to be a waffly twat, may your souls be judged accordingly.

Persephone Dedication:

To all my feminine peeps out there. This dedication is for you. Persephone is the Goddess of Spring and the Queen of the Underworld. I feel like that should be how every feminine peep should feel. Embrace your inner Persephone. Be gentle and loving, but don't be afraid to become dark and kick some ass when needed. Kindness is not a weakness. And to those who wish to tear us down, may you be on the edge of orgasm but never obtain it.

D - Districts. Sometimes known as 'cities' depending on where you are. A mayor rules each District.

States have merged together to form Territories. These Territories are divided into; Northeast Republic, Southeast Republic, Lakes of the North, Northwest Federation, Mountain Federation, Pacific Republic, and Texas. Alaska and Hawaii were able to avoid infiltration by the new world. They are no longer part of the United States.

A President rules the new America, and his council is comprised of each Territory Governor.

Contents

Prologue

Ten years. It has taken ten long years to take over this state. We took over our city in less than five years, but we needed the entire state. Every police officer, politician, city official, and anyone else with power is now under our control. Everyone except the governor, but that will come in time. All good things come to those who wait and all that shit. My brothers and I now rule what we call the Underworld, and we will rain hellfire down upon those who stand against us. Hades, Cerberus, Charon, and Thanatos are in control, and we look forward to finally seeing our girl again. She's our queen, our goddess, our Persephone. We did this all for her. We are her demons to rule and use as she wishes. She just doesn't know it yet.

Chapter One

JACE

Ten years ago . . .

At fourteen, I didn't really understand the term "heartbreak." How could a heart break? I thought it was just a stupid term. I . . . was wrong.

"Hey, J!"

I look up and smile at the blonde-haired, blue-eyed girl running toward us. My brothers, well brothers by choice, and I stand by our tree house waiting for her. I lift my hand in greeting. The tiny ten-year-old is a feisty little thing, but my brothers and I vowed to protect her a year ago when she stumbled across our treehouse covered in bruises. Her father is a grade-A douchecanoe who really needs to be put in jail. But unfortunately, he's the mayor of our town. No one will go against him when he has every police officer and gang member in his pocket. So a couple of kids vowed to protect her. We've managed so far.

"Hey, Moonbeam!" Alec says beside me. She rolls her eyes but smiles as she makes her way to us.

"How long can you stay, Starlight?" Howe asks as he makes his way up the tree ladder.

She purses her lips. "I still don't understand the weird nicknames."

"Maybe one day we'll explain, Sunshine." Zane laughs as he follows Howe.

She rolls her eyes and says, "Whatever. Anyway, my dad is staying out until about eight tonight. He said I needed to be home by then."

I bristle at her tone. "What's that supposed to mean?"

She shrugs as she reaches for the first step to climb up. "Not sure. He just said I had to be there by eight."

I grunt as I start up the stairs, with Alec following behind me. We all make ourselves comfortable and settle in. We spent the rest of the day playing games and laughing, not realizing that our whole world was about to change.

I watch as she makes her way down the stairs of the tree house. She looks up and smiles when she sees all four of us looking down at her. "I'll see you guys tomorrow," she says with a laugh, then heads back to her house. I huff out a sigh.

"What's up with you, man?" Zane questions as I return to my spot on the beanbag and fall on it.

I shrug. "Not sure. I just have a bad feeling." Eight o'clock rolls around, and I suddenly hear banging and yelling. I jump up and rush over to the window facing Jane's house. A bunch of hooded figures surround the house, and I watch as her father drags her out of their home. "Fuck!" I swear as the others jump up around me. I turn and rush to the tree house entrance, jumping for the swing rope and sliding down to the ground. As I run toward her, the others rush out behind me. "Jane!"

She looks up, and fear spreads across her face. "Jace! No, stop!" she screams.

I ignore her as I run. I hear grunts behind me and briefly look over my shoulder. My brothers fought the men and now have them pinned on the ground. I pause. "Shit," I grunt out.

Howe looks up at my voice, grunting as he fights. "Don't fucking stop on our account! Get our fucking girl!"

Nodding, I continue running toward our girl. I almost get to her, and she holds out her hand while fighting her father's grasp. My hand almost grasps hers; I'm so close. Out of nowhere, a man comes out of the darkness to grab me, and I don't see him coming until it's too late. My hand misses hers as I'm thrown to the side. I see the tears fall from her eyes as she resigns herself to whatever happens next. She smiles, and I barely hear the words as she whispers, "Thank you."

I yell and scream as I'm held on the ground, fighting with everything I am to get to our girl. To get to our light. She's the only good thing in our lives. We promised to protect her! We promised to be her protectors! We promised! I watch helplessly as she is tossed into the back of a car. She throws herself against the rear window, and I hear her screaming, "Don't hurt them! Please! Don't hurt them!"

I thrash on the ground, trying to get to her, even as the car pulls away. Suddenly, the weight on me is lifted. Before I can turn around to fight the guy who held me down, he's gone. Every single person who was just here is gone, except for my brothers walking toward me. I look back in the car's direction, hoping this is just a bad dream. For this nightmare to end. This isn't real. It can't be. I feel a shoulder brush against mine, and I turn to find Zane looking at me. He seems so lost.

"What are we going to do?" he asks quietly.

I look back in the direction of the missing car. That's when I realize that this isn't a nightmare. This is real. Our Moonbeam. Our Starlight. Our Sunshine. She's gone. Our light is gone. Snuffed out. My vision becomes blurry. Heartbreak is real. That's the only way I can describe the utter pain in my chest. The feeling of someone slowly shredding my heart into pieces. Heartbreak is real, and I know my brothers feel it too.

Chapter Two

JANE

10 years later...

Fuck! I rummage through my bag, trying to find my maps. I have to find them! On them, I've written down every place I have looked for my boys after running away from my father. He wanted to sell me off to the highest bidder to get pregnant, so he would have a male heir to take over for him. Instead, I said fuck you and left once I graduated from school. He has certainly made something of himself over the years, finally becoming the governor of our territory. He's had some competition, though. The rulers of the Underworld have taken over the territory, and word on the street is they are coming after him. I'd tip my hat off to them if I had one. I do odd jobs here and there to make enough money to travel around this Territory. Most I'm not proud of, but others have given me the tools to live independently and survive.

I finally find the map I was looking for and pull it out. Looking around, I notice I'm on the edge of Districts One and Two of the New York Territory, also known as the Atlantic Republic, but whatever. I sigh when I realize I have officially looked everywhere in New York for my boys. Grumbling, I shove the map back into my bag and heave it over my shoulder. Looking around, I pause when something on the electronic billboard catches my eye. Hum. I read the small words. "If you wish to for an audience with

Hades, follow the UV skulls." What? I look around, and that's when I notice the random UV lights throughout the city. Should I follow them?

Before I can think better about it, I follow the skulls. They lead me to a tavern. Odd location to set up an audience, but whatever. If anyone can find my boys, it would be them. They have their fingers in everything and are slowly branching into the surrounding territories. Steeling myself, I open the doors of the cavern and look around. It's a bit dusky but warm. There is a bar maiden in the corner washing cups. I head in her direction and sit on the stool facing her. I sigh before I say, "I need an audience with Hades." Way to just get to the point there, Jane. Fuck!

Looking up, she raises a brow. "Is that so?" She eyes me up and down before smirking. "You willing to pay the price?" she asks.

That has my brow rising. "What price?"

She grins as she walks over to a slick, black cell phone with the Hades symbol. "He's going to have fun with you, little girl." Her words make me bristle; I'm not a fucking little girl. A low, sexy male voice answers after a few rings. I can't hear what he's saying, but I can hear the bar maiden's side of the conversation. "Hello to you too, Charon. I have a girl here who wishes for an audience with Hades." She pauses for a moment before continuing, "I didn't ask her name. I didn't know it was necessary." She huffs out a sigh. "I don't fucking know! She's probably twenty or so."

My eyes widen. This is getting interesting. Finally, she looks back at me and asks, "What's your name, girl?"

I roll my eyes. No one goes against the men who run the Underworld, and I'm not about to get on their bad side when I need their help. I sigh and reply, "Jane." She repeats the name over the phone but rolls her eyes. Looking at me again, she grumbles, "Last name, dear?"

Well, this gets even more interesting. "Alexander. Jane Alexander." She repeats the name over the line, and I wish I could hear the other side of the conversation because her eyes look like they are about to bug out of her head. But then she looks back over at me, licking her lips.

"Very well, Ferryman. I'll let her know she needs to stay here till you arrive. Is there a time to expect you, sir?" She nods at his answer and lays the phone down beside her as she stares at me.

I raise a brow, slightly uncomfortable by her constant staring. "What?" I ask, slightly more aggressively than I meant to.

She just shakes her head. "Fuck, girl! I don't know what you did to get on their radar, but good-fucking-luck! Anyway, he will be here in about twenty minutes to take you to the caves." She sets a shot of whisky in front of me, arching a brow in question. Rolling her eyes, she says, "If you are old enough to fight for our country, you're old enough to drink is my motto. Plus, you are going to need it." She walks off, cleaning the tavern while I wait in silence.

Exactly twenty minutes later, there is a knock at the tavern door, and it opens. I jump slightly at the knock but turn in my chair to see who this Charon is. Holy. Fucking. Shit. Is all I can think because this dude is fucking fine! Not many men can pull off silver hair, but it looks incredible on him with his slightly tanned skin. His hair is styled in an angular comb-over, leaving a few strands to fall in front of his face. His eyes make me pause my ogling because, holy mother-of-pearl, they are entirely black with a red slit down the middle. They must be those colored sclera lenses. He also has a black hoop in his right eyebrow. A glint catches my eye, and that's when I notice the diamond studs in his ears. Mhm. Sexy. I continue my perusal down his body to find him wearing a white button-up with the sleeves cuffed at his forearm and a black vest with a red tie. I bite the inside of my cheek, trying not to smile because, man, that shirt is hugging him in all the right places. He has to be ripped under there, and his black slacks make me wonder if they embrace his ass too. I look back up at his face; he's got a brow raised and is trying not to grin. I just shrug.

He smirks slightly before saying, "I'm here to deliver you to Hades as requested."

Pulling myself off the stool, I lift my shot glass to the bar maiden with a smile. "Thanks for the drink." She nods to me and then bows her head slightly to Charon. We walk out the door and find an aqua Dodge Challenger parked in front. I let out an appreciative whistle. He opens the passenger door for me, and I slide inside. Damn, these guys sure know how to ride in style. I turn toward him as he starts the car. "So what's this price I have to pay?"

He asks, "Who said anything about a price?"

I point back at the tavern. "The lady inside said I would have to pay the price."

He grunts. "Yes, well, she tends to deal with less than moral people when it comes to an audience with Hades."

Narrowing my eyes at him, I ask, "So, no price then?"

He lets out a gruff laugh. "Oh, there will be a price. Nothing you won't be willing to give, I'm sure." I wait for him to elaborate, but he doesn't. So I turn to face forward, trying to psych myself up as much as possible before I enter the Underworld. Fuck, I hope I didn't make a huge mistake! Looking at Charon out of the corner of my eye, I hold my breath for a few seconds before letting it out. Maybe I should pray that I don't die? Hum. Fuck that shit. Praying never helped me before.

Chapter Three

JANE

Sitting silently in the front seat, I'm forced to deal with all the thoughts running through my brain, constantly playing tug-of-war with whether or not this is a good idea. Thoughts of the guys funnel through, and I grin. I can only imagine what the guys would think now if they were here. Jace would probably be screaming at me. He would tell me that this was a horrible idea and to call him immediately so he could pick me up. Howe would be even worse, yelling at Jace to bring him as backup in case they need to kick anyone's ass. I can't stop myself from giggling softly.

"What are you giggling about over there?" The gruff voice enters my thoughts, and I jump, coming back to the present. I turn to find my driver looking briefly at me before facing the road again.

I clear my throat. "Um, nothing." He raises a brow at me, and I huff a sigh. Then, realizing I am not going to get out of this, I decide to tell him half the truth. Better than the whole truth, right? "I was just thinking about my friends. Well, I suppose they aren't exactly my friends anymore." He grunts and nods for me to continue. Seriously? I'm just supposed to open up to this random guy I have never met? Fuck, Howe would have my head for this. "Not much else to say."

He turns to me, a question on his face. "I doubt that very much. There's something you want from us, correct? We will get to know each other very well if we decide to accept." I sneak a peek at him and see a hint of mischief in his gaze. Ugh, he reminds me of Alec. He would always get into trouble for practicing martial arts on the other guys. I smile at the memory.

I grunt as I say, "I was thinking about what my friends would say if they knew I got into a car with a stranger, heading to the headquarters of the gang that runs this territory. You are basically the mafia." I see the corner of this mouth tilt in a grin.

"And what would they say?" he asks with a hint of amusement.

Without thinking, I mutter, "Well, Jace would scream at me and say I'm asking to be kidnapped." Fuck, did I seriously just say his name? Fuck it. I suppose they will need to know their names to find them. I notice a hint of surprise light up his face before he quickly shuts it down.

"The others?" he asks. I stare at him a bit longer, wondering why he looks surprised but shake my head to clear the thought. I must be seeing things. I shrug as I continue, "Howe would volunteer to beat your ass if you hurt me. Um . . . Zane would just stand there looking intimidating, I suppose, but he would be Howe's backup. And," I pause at the thought of Alec. A smile takes over my face thinking about him because he was my teddy bear, the one who always held me when I cried. The one who would nurse me back to health after my dad beat me. His foster dad did horrible things to him, which I think was why we bonded so quickly. We helped each other through the pain. I'm pulled out of my thoughts again by Charon's deep voice. "What?"

He clears his throat. "You said and. And what?"

Taking a deep breath, I say, "Alec. Alec would be there to hold me if anything happened. He was my teddy bear, the one I always relied on not to freak out when I burst into tears." I laugh as a memory pops into my head. "The others would always run around trying to figure out who had hurt me and who they needed to kick around. But Alec, Alec would tell them to shut up. He would take me into their tree house and just hold me." I feel a little depressed now that I'm thinking about them. "I miss them,"

I whisper. A calloused hand gently rests on my thigh. I look up into those creepy sclera lenses but feel only comfort when I meet his soft gaze and smile.

"I'm sure they miss you too," he states confidently. Fuck, I wish I held that same conviction. I squeeze the hand on my thigh, trying to soak in his confidence.

"You think so?" I try not to sound needy as fuck, but damn. I really hope they have been looking for me as hard as I've been looking for them. The only problem was I couldn't make too much noise when searching because it would tip my father off to where I was. I've been looking for the last four years due to graduating early. I know my dad is looking for me, so I've been jumping from place to place, hoping I would find my guys in the process. Charon squeezes my thigh again.

"Why wouldn't they miss you? You make it sound like you were close." He lifts a brow in question.

I sigh and try to explain, "The closest. They are my best friends. Well, they were my best friends. Just wish I'd found them, or they'd found me already. Maybe they weren't even looking for me. Or maybe something happened to them." I shudder at the thought. He returns his hand to the steering wheel, making me miss the warmth his hand provided.

"Well, if I were one of them." He gives me a wink, and I laugh. "I would say that we looked all over America for you. Of course, we were also afraid that something had happened to you. But not to worry because we won't stop looking till we figure it out."

I soak in his assurance and feel determination fill my bones. He's right! I nod, encouraged by his words. "You're right. I can't give up!" I fist pump the air! Out of the corner of my eye, I notice him grin and feel my cheeks heat.

"Who knows, you may find them sooner than you think," he says as he parks the car outside a cave and turns to me. "Now, off to the meeting."

I nod, unbuckling myself. Opening the car door, I steel myself, trying not to lose the morale I've gained in the last few seconds. Charon comes up beside me, holding his elbow out. I thread my arm through his, thinking the action a bit odd, but what-the-fuck-ever. He leads me over to the entrance of the cave. Opening a door, we glide around. I can feel my heart beat faster with each step I take, and I hope to whatever higher power is watching me that Charon cannot hear it. He leads me through a maze of hallways and then opens another door, guiding me into an ultraviolet-lit room. He leads me into the center of the space and stops in front of a gentleman sitting on what looks like a throne; his head tilted down.

"Jane Alexander. Here to request an audience with Hades," Charon announces. I glance up at him and gasp. Holy fucking shit. He has a UV tattoo that covers half of his face. It's a skeleton. Fuck, that makes his eyes even more creepy. I hear the shuffle of feet, look in that direction, and notice another man dressed in what looks like an Assassin's Creed outfit. He has the hood up, covering the top half of his face. He also has a UV skeleton tattoo, but unlike the first man, it only covers the lower half of his face. I feel a brush of hot breath on my neck and squeak. At the noise, the man I was looking at lifts his head. I notice he has white sclera lenses. "That's Thanatos," Charon whispers in my ear.

I nod quickly, turning back to the gentleman on the throne. Another man stands beside him. He looks at home in the darkness with his milk chocolate skin tone and seems to have no issue showing off his muscular body in his medieval-meets-steampunk vest and fingerless leather gloves. His eyes show off three-eyed sclera lenses, and he also has a UV skeletal face tattoo. But his is different. Instead of normal skeletal teeth, his look sharp, like canine teeth. "That's Cerberus. While he doesn't have three heads, he has six eyes to make up for it." I had to appreciate the amount of effort put into his well-thought-out persona.

I turn my gaze back to Hades as he lifts his head and let out an audible gulp. Fuck! He has medium-length, black hair that meets his chin on one side and is short on the other, allowing me to see the snake earring that climbs up his earlobe. A skull eyebrow ring peeks out between the hair falling across his face. Seems they all have their faces tattooed because this guy has a full-face UV tattoo. His black sclera lenses make him look every inch the part of Hades. Dark and intimidating. He leans into his palm, and I notice his hands are also UV tattooed to depict skeletal fingers.

"Jane Alexander, what can we do for you?" His husky but authoritative voice rolls over me, and I have to suppress a shudder. Fuck, what have I gotten myself into?

Chapter Four

JANE

Standing there stiff in the middle of the Underworld headquarters, all I can think is fuck, why the hell did I think this was a good idea? But then I feel a hand squeeze my forearm. That's when I notice I still have my arm threaded through Charon's elbow. I look him in the eyes, and he winks at me. I let out a nervous giggle, covering my mouth with my free hand. Then I feel him lean down beside me and whisper, "Just breathe and tell him why you are here."

I nod and take a deep breath. I've got this! I'm surrounded by four extremely attractive and scary as fuck guys who run the whole Territory of New York. They are basically the mafia. I've got this! No reason whatsoever to be scared. I groan at my internal monologue. Wiping my free hand against my jeans to hopefully get rid of the moisture, I take a deep breath. "So, I asked for an audience to see if you could help find a few men for me?"

He raises a brow. "A few men?"

I nod as I continue, "Four, to be exact." He sits up now, seeming more interested.

"And what makes you think we can find these men for you?" he asks while tapping a ringed finger on the edge of his throne. I notice it's a black snake.

I shrug. "I haven't had any luck due to the fact that I can't make much noise in the area. So I figure you could make the noise for me."

He hums. "I see. And what makes you think these men want to be found?"

Looking up at Charon beside me, he nods, encouraging me to continue. I bite my lip, kneading it between my teeth as I think. He has a point, though. Maybe the guys don't want to be found. No. No! The guys wouldn't leave me behind. I had to believe that. Steeling myself, I look Hades in the eyes. "They wouldn't leave me behind. They would want to find me. So if they can't find me, I want to find them. But I have been trying to locate them on my own for the last four years with no success. I need help." I really hope the pleading in my voice didn't sound as bad as it did in my head.

He nods. "Very well. What are their names?"

As I answer, I try to suppress the hope rising in my chest. "Jace Miller, Zane Masters, Alec Moore, and Howe Taylor." There's a visible shift in the room when I finish. I'm not entirely sure what's changed, but I can feel it. It's like all the air has been sucked out of the room. Hades shifts in his seat and sits up tall.

He grins as he says, "Very well. But I must ask for payment before we look for your men."

I stiffen but nod. I was expecting this. "What is the payment you require?"

He stands from his throne and saunters toward me, his voice dark as he says, "You become ours."

I raise a brow as I sputter, "I become yours?" I look around the room to find the other two men closing in as Charon tightens his hold on me. "You're serious? Like . . . all of yours?"

"Oh, he's serious, Starlight," the milk chocolate male says beside Hades. I stiffen at the nickname. Cerberus, that was his name. Only one person has ever called me that, and I haven't heard his voice in ten years. No one is allowed to call me that except for him. Only Howe.

Glaring at him, I growl and say, "Only one person is allowed to call me that. So, what's with the weird nickname?"

A gravelly, gruff voice speaks up beside him, "Maybe one day we will explain it to you, Sunshine."

I gasp, closing my eyes. No. No. No. No. It can't be true! Zane used to say that every single time I asked that question. I look over my shoulder at Charon, and he winks at me again. "Speechless there, Moonbeam?" I choke on a sob. Alec. My Alec. I gaze at the male in front of me, and he grins. I shake my head, unable to believe what is happening. Blinking fast, I try to clear my blurry vision, but it's no use.

"J," I whisper, not wanting to hope, but damn, my heart is painfully throbbing with it.

"Hey, Princess," he says softly. That's when I break and fall to my knees. My guys. My boys are here in front of me!

Chapter Five

JACE/HADES

Fuck! I wasn't expecting the waterworks. Tears. I fucking hated them when I was younger, and obviously, I didn't grow out of that. Don't get me wrong, I've made many women cry in my line of work. Doesn't bother me one bit. But Jane? Jane's different. I look at the other guys. I can see the panic in Howe's and Zane's eyes as I shift my gaze over to Alec, who just rolls his eyes at us. He's always been the one who could handle her tears, not us! I'm ripped from my thoughts when she flings her body against me and wraps her arms around my neck. I stand there shocked for a few seconds but begin to relax the longer I hold Jane in my arms. I have to admit, she was a cute thing when we were younger, but puberty did great things for her.

She still has hypnotizing gray-blue eyes, but she now comes up to my chin. Which would make her about five-six or so. She's filled out and has some thickness to her. It makes me happy to see she's no longer the thin child she was when we were younger. Thick but toned. Sexy as hell. I tangle my fingers into her now pastel, prism-colored hair. I feel my body trying to betray me. Focus! Fuck! You have a crying woman in your arms, Jace. I'm brought back when I hear her soft voice in my ear, "I fucking missed you."

Holding her tighter, I whisper back, "I missed you too, Princess." I hear her wet snort at the nickname. I only got away with using it once in a while when we were kids. She hated when I called her princess because she thought that meant she couldn't take care of herself. I would laugh and tell her she was a warrior princess. After that, I got away with it more often. The standard lights flick on instead of the UV lights, and I have to blink a few times so my eyes can adjust. I look over Jane's head and notice Alec walking back over. He must have walked over to the corner of the room to switch the lights when she launched herself at me. Once her sobs quiet down, she pulls away and wipes her eyes.

"Your eyes are still creepy as hell in normal lighting," she says with a laugh. I pull out my contact case and carefully pluck my lenses out. I look back up, noticing the others doing the same.

I grin at her. "Better?" She reaches up, and her fingers glide beside my slightly tilted eyes. Without the lenses, she can see my dark brown eyes, which look almost black. Compliments of my Chinese mother, or so I've been told. I wouldn't know because my brothers and I grew up in the same foster home since we were kids. She nods, looking over to Howe beside me.

With a grin, she teases, "I see you're still a troublemaker."

Howe laughs, opening his arms wide for her. I can see the laughter in his light hazel eyes as she pounces on him, and he swings her around while she laughs. I smile at them. I haven't seen him this happy in what feels like forever. He stops swinging her and places a kiss on the top of her head, which he can easily do, being a foot taller than her.

Giving her a tight hug, he whispers, "Always, Starlight. I've missed you so much."

She squeezes him back. "Me too, big guy." She pulls away from Howe, looking to Zane next. She pauses when she notices that his hood is still hiding his face. I run a hand through my hair in worry. He doesn't want to show her the damage to his left eye. It's my fault he had to protect me when we took over the city. He got jumped during a fight when we were eighteen, and he's partially blind out of that eye now. His voice never recovered from almost being choked to death, leaving him with a deep, gravelly voice. It helps with the intimidation factor when dealing with clients, but for the most part, it just reminds me of my fuckup.

"Hey, Zane?" she whispers. He releases a deep breath before pulling off the hood. Rubbing a hand through his long, chocolate hair, he flips the ends out, making the red tips disappear behind his back. He takes another deep breath before lifting his gaze to meet hers. I can tell she notices that one of his ice-blue eyes is more glazed over when she gasps. She rushes over to him, lifting her hand to hover over the scar. He gives her a small tilt of his lips, making his snake-bite piercing glint in the light. Placing a hand over hers, he presses it against his cheek.

"I'm fine, Sunshine. It happened a long time ago." His voice comes out gruff from lack of use today. "Missed you too, by the way. Don't want you thinking these guys were the only ones." She lets out a laugh before encircling his torso and giving him a tight hug.

Lastly, she looks over at Alec. "I knew there was something familiar about you on the car ride here." He grins at her, opening his arms wide. His golden-brown eyes glisten with happiness at finally having her back. She rushes to him, wrapping her arms around him and resting her head against his chest. He tightens his hold on her. "It was so hard not to tell you in the car."

"So why didn't you?" she whispers into his chest.

"The guys wanted to make sure you were who you said you were. I knew you were my Moonbeam the minute I saw you, but I wanted the guys to see you before we told you." He pulls away from her with another grin.

She turns in Alec's arms, facing me with a smile before saying, "Well, I suppose you found my boys a lot quicker than I originally thought you would."

I laugh as I say, "Your boys, huh?"

She grins and sasses back, "Yes, my boys. You got a problem with that, sir?"

The boys around me laugh when I let out a growl. "Sir?"

She steps away from Alec and makes her way back over to me. "Well, you are the boss around here, are you not?"

The minute she gets within reach, I grab her wrist and pull her to me. She places her hand against my chest, and I'm sure she can feel my heart pounding. Releasing her wrist, I wrap one arm around her waist and thread my fingers through her hair with my other hand. I stare into her gray-blue eyes, assuring myself she really is here. Her lips tilt into a smile, and I grin back as I reply, "Yes, I would say I'm the official boss around here. But the boys and I run this thing together."

"She still hasn't agreed to our price yet, Hades," Howe states beside me.

Right, I almost forgot. Still at work. I look down at Jane with a grin. "He's correct. You haven't agreed to our price yet."

She rolls her eyes. "You revealed yourselves before I could agree or not."

I grip her chin, forcing her to meet my eyes. "So what is your answer, Princess?" She tries to look at the others, but I refuse to release her chin. "We are waiting, Princess." She stares me down for what feels like forever before there is a slight tilt to her lips.

"I've always been yours."

Glancing up, I find the guys smiling. I pull away and bow slightly to her before looking into her eyes and proclaiming, "Then long live the Queen."

Chapter Six

JANE

I stand there shocked and in awe when I notice that the other guys are also bowing their heads slightly. "The Queen?" I repeat. What the hell are these boys talking about? Jace straightens in front of me, a smile on his face. Is it Jace or Hades? Fuck, I need to ask them about the names.

He smirks as he says, "You are now the Queen of the Underworld, Darling."

The way he says darling makes me want to shiver. I never really thought of my boys in a sexual way because, well, we were kids back then, but damn, the way he growls my name turns me on. Fuck! Get a hold of yourself, Jane! I mentally slap myself. You seriously just got your boys back, and now you're inserting them into a sexual fantasy! Focus on what's important right now! I try to remember what he just said. Queen of the Underworld. The Underworld? Fuck, does he mean the entire empire they built? "I'm the Queen of the Underworld?" I ask in disbelief.

Jace laughs. He shrugs and says, "Well, you are the Persephone to my Hades. Seems only fitting."

I arch a brow. "Persephone?" Howe steps up beside me, grinning.

"We all have code names and use them when working. No one knows our real names. Well, except for you. We only use our real names when we are at home. But we spend most of our time here at the cave," Howe explains and shrugs.

"So I shouldn't use your real names here or in public? Just when we are at your house?" I ask.

Howe nods. "It will be your house now too."

I freeze at the thought. I'll be living with them now? The idea doesn't freak me out as much as I think it should. I'm more surprised at the thought of actually having a house to call home. But wait, they said they spend most of their time here. "But you said you spend most of your time here. Where do you sleep when you're here?"

I feel a presence step up behind me and look over my shoulder to find Zane and Alec. Wait, should I still call them Thanatos and Charon in my head so I don't accidentally say their real names out loud? Fuck, this is getting confusing! I massage my temples, trying to stave off the headache I feel coming on. "Actually, before you guys start answering questions, can we go somewhere safe where I can say your names? I'm too shocked to keep real names versus code names from popping out of my mouth." The guys laugh, and Jace shrugs.

"Sure. I need to let the Hellhounds know who you are anyway, so they don't think you're a threat." He turns, walking to the door I entered through. With a smile, Howe grabs my hand, threading his fingers through mine and guiding me to follow.

My brows furrow. "Hellhounds?"

Alec threads his fingers through my other hand and gives it a soft squeeze. "They're our guards. Had to continue with the Underworld theme we have."

I nod and glance behind me, wondering where Zane is. Finding him directly behind me has me jumping. I hear him snicker and growl at him, not seeing them scaring me funny at all. I silently follow behind Jace with the guys. It's a few minutes before we enter another room. As we enter, I gasp. This time, Howe snickers beside me, and I elbow him. This room is every computer nerd's wet dream. It has to be the room Howe spends most of his time in. When we were younger, he was really into cybersecurity and hacking. There are monitors everywhere, and I can see every inch of the cave compound from here. I watch as Jace makes his way over to a high-tech walkie-talkie.

He brings the device to his mouth and says, "Attention, Hellhounds. This is Hades. We have a new member in the Underworld compound. Persephone has arrived. I expect the same protections to be given to her as you have given to us. I need Alpha and Beta to the security room to be briefed." After he is done talking, there's a pause before two distinct people reply, "Affirmative," over the comms. He nods and places the walkie-talkie back on what looks like a charger before leaning against the desk.

"How long do you think it will take them to get here?" Howe asks beside me. I quirk a brow in question, but they ignore it. That's fine. I don't know what the hell is going on anyways. I snort at the unintentional underworld pun.

Zane walks over to stand beside Jace and shrugs. "Shouldn't take too long. They just did a perimeter check about five minutes ago." Just as he finishes, two men walk through the door. They both look young, but the gasp that escapes my mouth isn't due to that. No, it's due to their fucking eyes!

I lift a finger, pointing at them. "What the fuck is wrong with their eyes?!" The guys beside me burst out laughing, and I look over to find Zane grinning as he tries not to laugh with the others. I turn to the two men who walk in smiling. "What?!" I screech. "It's a totally reasonable question! Their fucking eyes are glowing like a fucking cat's!" The two men pull out what look to be matching pairs of glasses from their sleeve pockets and cover their creepy eyes.

Jace is still grinning as he comes up beside me. "First, Alpha, Beta, this is Persephone. Persephone, meet Alpha and Beta. Alpha is the one to your left with the A on his shoulder. He is the head of security and the boss of my

Hellhounds. Beta is to your right with the B on his shoulder. He is second in charge. When Alpha isn't here, Beta is in charge of everything." He turns to his men. "I expect you to explain to the others what she looks like and who she is so there is no confusion."

Both men nod. "Yes, Hades," they say in unison.

Jace turns back to me and grins. "As for the eyes, Darling, they are high-tech contacts. They allow my men to see in the dark. It's why most of the hallways have low lighting. They also spend much of their time in the darker parts of the compound for security purposes. The glasses they now have on allow them to see even with all the bright lights in the room." He shrugs. "Think of the contacts like night vision goggles. They allow my men to do their jobs without oversized equipment preventing them from proper movement in a life-or-death situation."

"So, why were their eyes glowing when they came in?"

Howe bumps my side and answers, "It was the reflection of the contacts that created the glow. We also provide contacts that change color when they are outside in the sun. Their eyes will look almost black because of them. We try to ensure our people have the best technology on their side so that they can do their jobs properly."

I nod, thinking about it. That makes sense. If the guards can see in the dark at night and in the light during the day, that would make it hard for enemies to sneak into this compound. I still think their eyes looked creepy, though. I'm sure they look weird during the day too. I go to clap my hands together, a nervous habit of mine when I feel awkward, but realize that I am still holding Alec's and Howe's hands. Well, now I feel even more uncomfortable. I groan, then ask, "Okay. Well, can we find somewhere to talk now that I feel thoroughly awkward?" The two guards bow and leave the room. The guys grin but don't comment on my outburst as we make our way down the hallway and some stairs. We immediately turn down a hallway to our right and enter the first room on the right.

As we step into the room, I immediately stop and take in the space. This is not one of the guys' rooms; it doesn't match any of their personalities. It's decorated with deep red and black fabrics that cover the cave walls. Moroccan lanterns cover the ceiling that leads to a large Moroccan chandelier in the center of the room. The light from it throws delicate patterns around the room. I release the guys' hands as I walk farther into the space. Looking to my right, I see a bathroom and run over to investigate. I find that the Moroccan theme has also carried into here. Dropping my gaze to the floor, I notice that the floors don't match the ones in the hallways. The flooring in the bedroom and bathroom is made up of deep red and black hexagonal tiles. It's fucking beautiful. The bathroom holds a large vanity, and I notice a deep-pink crown sitting on it by the sink. I smile as I continue to browse. There is a large black soaker tub in the corner that I bet is perfect for relaxing. They made a room for me. They hadn't seen me since I was ten, yet they believed they would find me. They believed so much that they made a room for me. I take a deep breath, trying to get my emotions under control, and turn to see the guys crowding around the bathroom doorway. "I'm assuming this room isn't one of yours, considering the pink crown on the counter," I tease. They all grin at me as Zane walks toward me.

"This is definitely not one of our rooms, Sunshine." He stops in front of me. Reaching out slowly, he pushes a strand of prism-colored hair behind my ear. I nuzzle into his hand. Doubt creeps into my head when I think about how long we have been apart. Maybe this room wasn't for me. Did it belong to another girl? Should I ask?

Taking a deep breath and dropping my eyes to the floor, I whisper, "Did it belong to one of your girlfriends?" I feel him gently brush his thumb across my cheek. Fuck, I don't want to know the answer. Why did I even ask?! Thinking about them with other girls hurts my heart in a way I never thought possible. Of course, they were with other women, Jane! You were only friends! It's not like you were romantically involved with these guys.

Then why does it feel like my heart is tearing in four different directions? Fuck. Jane, you are not allowed to fall in love with your best friends. Yes, I said I would be with them, but that doesn't mean romantically. Right? I can feel my eyes starting to burn. No! NO! Don't fucking cry again!

"Sunshine? Look at me." I shake my head, refusing to look up. No. I know the minute I do, the tears will fall, and I refuse to cry over something as stupid as them having previous girlfriends. He releases his hold on my face, and I want to whimper at the loss until he pulls me into his chest and wraps his arms around me. I take a deep breath, and his musky smell surrounds me. He smells woodsy and smoky. I take a few more deep breaths and start to calm down. "We made this room for you and only you," he whispers.

Hearing the others come in, I squeeze myself tighter against Zane. Stupid fucking tears. "I didn't expect you guys to be saints," I manage to say between hiccups. He holds me even tighter. I feel someone come up beside me and join in the hug, and I hiccup out a laugh because I know it's Howe. Alec places himself on my other side, leaving Jace at my back.

I feel him rest his forehead against the back of my head. He sighs and says, "I'm not going to lie to you and say we were saints while we searched for you." I huff. I'm not angry, and the hurt isn't as painful as I thought it would be hearing him say that. Maybe it's because he's not trying to hide it. "But I want to make one thing clear, Darling." He moves so his lips are right by my ear. "Though you may be ours, we are just as much yours. We built this empire for you and only you. You are our Queen, always have been, and always will be."

Chapter Seven

JANE

The guys had left me alone to enjoy some time in my new room. Now that I'm sitting on my bed, I'm slightly flushed, thinking about what happened in the bathroom. That was somewhat embarrassing. Why the hell would I ask them about other women? Falling back onto the bed, I let out a deep sigh. Grumbling to myself, I burrow under the black and red comforter. It's been a while since I've even had a bed, let alone somewhere comfortable to sleep. I'm pulled from rambling thoughts by a snickering sound, and my eyes fly open when I realize I'm no longer alone in the room. Fuck! I guess they didn't want to leave me alone for long. As I slowly lift my head, I find all the guys standing at the edge of my bed. I didn't even hear them come in. I notice Alec is covering his mouth as if to smother the snicker he already let out. I raise a brow in question.

He shrugs. "You were burrowing into the bed like a little kitten." I feel my cheeks heat in embarrassment. He grins as he says, "It's cute, Moonbeam."

"Well, I haven't had a bed this nice in years," I grumble and reply, letting my head fall back onto the bed. The bed bounces beside me, and I turn to find Howe lying on his belly a few inches away from my face.

He grins before saying, "He didn't mean anything by it, Starlight." I roll my eyes. In response to my eye roll, someone lets out a deep, primal growl in front of my face. My eyes widen, and I can't help the shiver that races down my spine. I hear a quiet squeak on my other side and turn toward the noise to find Alec there, nibbling his lip with wide eyes. Turning back to Howe, I find his face still mere inches from mine. His light hazel eyes darken as a satisfied smirk takes over his face. Well. I'm going to have to investigate that later. Mhm. The possibilities. I'm brought out of my thoughts when I notice Howe's lips moving.

"Wait, what?"

He grins. "I was saying that maybe Alec needs to apologize since you thought he was making fun of you." He raises his eyes, then a brow to the male in question. I look back to Alec on my other side. Wow, I feel like a damn yo-yo flipping my head back and forth. I find Alec gaping like a fish. He opens and closes his mouth, looking slightly panicked. I can't help the giggle that erupts from me. He looks completely lost, almost as if Howe is reprimanding him instead of me. I hope this friendship comes with some benefits because I can see Howe and me having some fun with Alec, if you know what I mean.

At my giggling, Alec narrows his eyes at me. I flip onto my belly with a grin and army crawl over to him. I lay on my back and rest my head on his lap. Then, smiling up at him, I say, "Oh, get that frown off your face. You love me too much to stay mad at me." He rolls his eyes but starts running his fingers through my hair. I raise my hand and rub the frown line between his brows. "Plus, frowning will give you lines, and you are way too pretty to have frown lines." At that, he huffs out a laugh. The other guys move closer to us, and I close my eyes, enjoying the comforting feel of Alec's fingers running through my hair. I feel at home here, surrounded by my guys.

Who would have thought I would be here snuggling with my boys just a few moments after meeting Hades? Not me. I would have laughed in your face if you had told me this was how the night would turn out. I have my boys back. I have a bed. I have a bathtub. Oh! I have a bathtub! I moan at the thought. Fuck! A bath would be heavenly right now. Wait. Remembering that I don't have any clothes other than what's in my backpack, I groan.

"What the fuck are you moaning and groaning about over there, Princess?"

I open one eye, trying to pinpoint Jace's voice. "I was thinking about my less-than-adequate clothing choices. Also, I thought I was the Queen?" I grin at him. He gives me a look, but I catch the twitch of his lip.

He waves his hand as if dismissing what I said. "We will go shopping for clothes tomorrow." I watch as he crawls over the bed toward me. He keeps creeping closer till his face is hovering directly above mine. When I give an audible gulp, he gives me a wry smirk. "You are *our* Queen. You are *my* Princess." He lowers his face till our lips are so close that I think he may kiss me. His breath whispers across my lips as he says, "Darling, I'm in awe of your abundant love and forgiveness." I'm startled by his words and certainly too stunned to move. What's that supposed to mean? Abundant love? Does he feel it too? The chemistry that seems to have magically appeared in just the short time I've been here? Or maybe we just built this reunion up in our heads, and the high is making me feel like there is something more than there really is. Ugh, I'm too much of a fucking coward to say anything because I don't want to ruin what we have going on right now. Is it love if I feel like my heart is about to explode? Internally cringing, I wonder what a girl who hasn't known love all her life has to offer. Do I even know what love is? I let out a sigh as Jace moves away.

"You can borrow some of our clothes for the night if you want to shower," Howe says at my feet. I nod at him, unsure if my voice will come out steady. He gives me a wink, gets off the bed, and heads out the door. Jace and Zane head toward the door as well. I'm about to call out to them, not even sure what I will say, but they stop and turn back toward me.

"Enjoy the rest of your night, Princess. See you in the morning." Jace leaves through the door, heading in the same direction as Howe.

"Rest, Sunshine. I'm sure this day has been overwhelming," Zane says as he heads out the door.

"Night, Zane," I call out before he disappears around the corner like the others. He gives me a grunt, and I can't help but smile. It's such a Zane thing to do. He never did well with emotions and mushy situations; it looks like that hasn't changed. I find Alec staring down at me, and I smile up at him as he brushes his fingers over my forehead. Mhm. My eyes flutter closed. I always loved when he did this when I was younger. I sigh, feeling my muscles slowly release the tension I've pent up over the last few years.

"Hey, Jane," he whispers.

"Mm?" I mumble back.

"Were you wanting to take a bath? Howe just returned with clothes and put them in the bathroom for you." He continues to ghost his fingers across my face.

"Mhm."

He softly laughs. "I can start the bath for you."

I grin up at him. "Sounds great." He gently removes my head from his lap, jumps up from the bed, and heads to the bathroom. I lie there for a few moments before I hear the rush of water. Grumbling to myself, I realize I now have to leave this comfortable bed. Rolling over, I hop off the bed and head to the bathroom. When I walk in, I find Alec hunched over the tub with his sleeves rolled past his elbows. He seems to be swirling the water around. "Whatcha doin?"

He turns to me with a smile. "I added some bath salts to the water." Rising from the ground, he grabs a washcloth from the cupboard beside the bath. Wiping off the excess water, he says, "I know you prefer lilac, but we currently don't have anything with that smell. I figured lavender would be okay, though. We can get more bath stuff tomorrow while we are out."

I grin, surprised he remembered my favorite scent. Lavender is a close second, though. I wrap my arms around his waist, holding him tight. "Thank you."

Embracing me, he kisses the top of my head. "It's just bath salts, Jane."

I tighten my hold on him and respond, "Thank you for coming to the tavern to get me. For leading me back to the others. For never giving up on finding me." My throat clogs with emotion because I don't think he realizes how much this means to me. How alone I felt without them. "For giving me a home," I whisper.

Placing his hand against my cheek, Alec forces me to look up at him. He looks so serious right now, his golden-brown eyes piercing me with their intensity. "You are our Queen. You always have been and always will be. We never stopped looking for you and never once thought to stop searching." He brushes his thumb under my eye, and I realize I've let the tears slip from my control. Fuck, I've never cried so much in my life. What are these guys doing to me? He kisses my forehead. "We will keep you safe, Jane. We won't let you slip through our fingers this time, understand?"

I nod, and he brushes his lips against my forehead before backing toward the door. I continue staring at the tub, trying to control my emotions. I really want to believe that they will keep me safe. I want to hope, above all hopes, that my father will never find me. But, I've found hope is fickle, and I've been burned too many times by her flames.

Chapter Eight

JANE

I'm frantically trying to find a way out of this dream. Running toward the only door I see as fast as I can. It slams shut, and I halt in the dark. This is only a dream. Only a dream. Maybe if I tell myself that enough, I will wake up.

"Daughter, where are you?"

Fuck! Nightmare! It's a nightmare! I can feel the scream in my throat, trying to find a way out, but I choke it down. This isn't real. I ran away from home. I've been on my own for years, looking for my guys. I'm with my guys now! Squatting down, I cover my ears and close my eyes. Maybe if I ignore what's happening, I'll wake up.

"My little girl. Jane, why are you hiding from Daddy? I want to show you something."

I squeeze my closed eyes tighter. No. NO! Just go away! Just go away! This isn't real. This isn't real!

"There you are. I've been looking all over the place for you. Come now, Jane. I have someone I want you to meet."

I don't move. Refusing to give in to this nightmare.

"Jane, don't make me repeat myself. You know what happens when I am forced to repeat myself."

I whimper at the thought. I feel ghostly fingers running through my hair and tears streaming down my face. I'm not sure if it's only in my nightmare *or if it's in the real world, but I want to wake up! The fingers tighten their hold, and I whimper from the pain.*

"Let's go, Jane." The dark promise in his voice tells me to get up and move, but my body isn't listening. The fingers tighten and jerk me out of my huddled position, pulling me along. I scream as I pull and scratch the hands holding onto my hair. "Now, now, Little Princess. You know how I hate repeating myself. Be a good girl and submit."

I scream and continue fighting his hold. I'm not a little girl anymore! I scream and scream till my throat hurts.

I'm about to faint in the dream when I feel the tug back to reality. I jerk awake with a scream, throwing the blankets off the bed. Looking around, I realize that the lanterns on the ceiling are softly lit, so I'm not surrounded by darkness. Gulping down air, I fall back onto the bed and cover my eyes. I feel the wetness on my face, which means I was also crying in the real world. A sob slips out that I can't hold back. I'm not sure if I'm crying over the nightmare or in relief that it wasn't real.

"Jane?"

I bite my lip, trying to stop my cries. Fuck, I woke the guys up. I can feel their stares from the doorway. Throwing my hand in the air, I wave them off. Taking a deep breath, I say, "I'm fine." A few minutes pass, and I think they may have left. Then the bed dips beside me. A sob escapes my lips, and I cover my face again. Gentle hands pry my hands away, but I refuse to look at whoever it is.

"Jane, look at me."

I shake my head, refusing. It's Alec, and if I look at him right now, I know I won't be able to hold back my sobs.

He draws gentle circles on my hand with his thumb to soothe me. "Please, Moonbeam. Look at me."

Taking a deep breath, I open my eyes. Tears slip down my cheeks as I do. He slowly leans over and brushes away the wetness. "Hey, you still look beautiful."

A snort of laughter bubbles out, but it doesn't stop the sob that follows.

He pulls on my hand, and I shimmy to him to crawl into his lap. He wraps his arms around me. I shove my face into the crook of his neck and inhale his familiar scent. He smells just like he did as a kid. Like smoke and fire. Warm. It's home. My mind and heart take that as a white flag of surrender, unleashing my pain, fear, and sorrow.

He rocks me from side to side as I'm wrought with debilitating sobs. My fingers dig into his back, trying to drag him even closer. I'm so afraid that if I let go, he will disappear. When I open my eyes, blurry as they may be, his lips are right there. "It's okay, Moonbeam. I got you. I have you, and I'm not letting go." He squeezes me tighter, pushing his cheek into my forehead. I feel cold liquid on my forehead as he does, making me cry harder. He's crying too. We would cry together as kids too. Sharing in each other's pain.

A hand rests on the top of my head, and I flinch. "It's me, Sunshine." I can hear the pain in Zane's voice, and he slowly pulls away.

"Please. Please, come back, Zane," I say between hiccups. I know he would never do anything to hurt me. His hand touches my head again and runs his fingers through my hair. I push my head into his touch, letting him know it's fine.

Two sets of hands start massaging my feet. I can tell who is who by their hands, even after all this time. Jace has my right foot, rubbing with long, delicate fingers. Fingers of a pianist. Howe has my left foot. His hands are larger with calluses. Surrounded by the guys, I feel myself relaxing and my panic falling away. My tears slowly subside, and I snuggle closer into Alec's hold.

Jace squeezes my foot and asks, "How are you feeling, Princess?"

I pull away to look at him. "Like I got hit by a Mack truck. Otherwise, I'm feeling better now."

Looking back up at Alec, I see his face is still wet with tears. I reach up and stroke my thumb across his cheek. He shudders, closing his eyes as he nuzzles his face against my palm.

"I missed you so much, Jane," he says quietly. When his eyes open, the golden-brown color seems to glisten from the tears he shed.

Shifting in his hold, I press my lips to his. Fuck! What the hell am I doing? It was a gut reaction! I jerk away, lowering my head in shame. "I'm sorry," I squeak.

I feel his fingers under my chin as he lifts my face. He glides them from underneath my chin to trail them across my cheek. He's searching my eyes for something, but I'm not sure what he's looking for. "Did you want to kiss me?" he asks.

I nip and pull at my lip while debating what to say. Pulling my lip from between my teeth with his thumb, he gently rubs his finger across it. "Did you want to kiss me?" he asks again.

"Yes," I whisper.

The smile he gives me is blinding. He leans down, places a soft kiss against my lips, then pulls away slightly and says, "I want to kiss you too." His lips are mere inches away from mine when he whispers, "Do you want to kiss the others?"

I groan. The thought of kissing all of them has my breathing quickening. The hands on my right foot tighten, and I pull away from Alec to look at Jace. His eyes flick to my lips and then back up to my eyes. His tongue peeks out as he licks his lips. I hear a deep growl as the hands on my left foot tighten. Switching my gaze to Howe, I see that his light-hazel eyes have darkened with desire. He shifts to his knees and crawls toward me.

Zane's hands stroking my hair have now tightened their hold, but it's different than how my father used to grab it. Instead, his touch is tender.

Zane promised he would never hurt me, and I could feel the truth behind those words. He gently tugs my head back, and my eyes meet his. Lowering his face so that his lips are next to my ear, he whispers, "I can tell you that I have dreamed about kissing you for years, Sunshine."

He shifts so his lips are a breadth away from mine, and I shiver at how aroused I'm getting. After so long apart, I never thought the boys I knew as kids could make me feel this way. They are slowly killing me with their soft kisses and touches. Zane nips at my lower lip and grins when I moan. "Be a good girl for the others. I, unfortunately, have to get up early for work." Before he pulls away completely, he presses his lips to mine. The kiss is not gentle like I thought it would be. Instead, it's dark and demanding. As if he's trying to memorize my lips. I whine as he pulls away and gives my hair one last tug. Then he leaves the room. Before I can lower my head, I feel another set of lips against my neck and hum my approval.

"Have fun with these boys, Princess," Jace says as he moves out from behind me so I can see him. He gives me a chaste kiss of his own, then says, "I want you all to myself next time, Princess." Giving me a wicked grin, he disappears from view.

There's a soft nibble on my neck, and I groan. The smell of leather and smoke surrounds me, an intoxicating mixture.

"It seems our Queen wants something, Howe." Alec teases as he nips my ear.

I feel Howe lick up my neck. Normally, I would think that's gross, but right now, it's making my nipples ache, and I'll need a new pair of underwear soon. "Is that right, Alec?" I lower my head, so I can finally look at Howe but notice he isn't looking at me. Instead, he's looking at Alec behind me.

Thoughts of them together enter my mind, and I shift, feeling wetness pool between my legs. Howe's eyes flick to mine, and almost as if he could hear my thoughts, he gives me a mischievous grin. Without taking his eyes off mine, he grabs the back of Alec's neck and pulls him into a kiss. I feel Alec stiffen behind me. Maybe he's afraid I'll judge. I grin. "Don't stop on my account." I grab Alec's hand and glide his fingers down my body to show him the evidence of how turned on I am from watching them. I glide his hand beneath the fabric of my clothes to my core, crying out in pleasure when his fingers glide over my clit. Fuck, it's been a while since I've had sex. I look back up to find them both still kissing, but Howe's eyes are on me. He grinds his hard length against my leg as Alec's fingers find their way inside me.

I groan again. Howe's eyes are filled with fire, making me grin. My hands aren't doing anything, so I glide my fingers across the top of his underwear. He pushes his lower half closer as I shimmy his underwear down. Once his dick is unbound, he groans into Alec's mouth. Alec adds another finger inside me, increasing his pace as his palm rubs my clit. I grin at the size of Howe. He is one LARGE glass of chocolate milk. And I do LOVE chocolate milk. I reach out and brush my finger across the tip of his cock, and he jerks at the touch. Wrapping my hand around his cock, I squeeze and pump him fast and hard.

He growls into Alec's mouth again as he pumps his hips into my hand. I try to coordinate the thrusts of his hips with my hand, rubbing the tip of his head every few pumps. I can tell he's getting close, but I don't want him to come like this. I halt Alec's hand with my own and stop pumping Howe. Alec pulls away from Howe to see the look on my face. He must understand what I want because he pulls away fully. Without Alec's mouth and my hand pumping him, Howe lets out a dark growl.

I grin as I push on his chest, and he falls back onto the bed. "What's up?"

Crawling across the bed till I'm right in front of him, I give him a smirk before sealing my lips around the head of his cock. "Oh! Fuck, yeah!" he yells.

I feel Alec behind me as he pushes my underwear aside and starts finger fucking me again. Oh, god, that feels good! I hum in pleasure. Howe rakes his fingers into my hair and grips it tightly as I hum. I grin around his cock. He seems to like the humming, so I hum again as Alec hits a pleasurable spot.

"Fuck! Alec, fuck yourself! Do it hard and fast," Howe orders as his hand gentles, then tightens again. His hips jerk up, and I almost gag. I power through it and hum around him again. Alec's breaths are coming faster now as he slams his fingers into me, and I cry out as an orgasm hits. Fuck! I wasn't even expecting it.

I continue to suck Howe's cock as I come down from my high. "Fuck!" he pants. "You're both so beautiful! God." His fingers tighten in my hair as he looks over my shoulder at Alec. Howe's eyes darken in pleasure as he says, "I bet your ass would be so tight too, Alec! God, I love fucking you!" Alec cries out behind me, and I feel hot ribbons of come hit my legs and back. Seems Howe's dirty talk did it for him. I hum one last time as I squeeze Howe's balls, and he roars as he comes into my mouth. I swallow every last drop and lick the tip of his cock one last time. Alec's fingers slip from my body, and I sit up.

Howe is lying there panting with a satisfied grin on his face. "Fuck, Jane."

Looking behind me, I find Alec in the same position. His eyes meet mine, and he smirks and says, "I don't think I've ever come that hard before."

"Hey!" Howe growls.

I laugh at Howe and smile at Alec. "Is that so?"

He shrugs. "I was seriously turned on by the two of you. I don't think my body knew what the fuck to do."

"So it's not something I'm doing wrong. Is that what you're saying?" Howe asks.

Alec rolls so he can crawl across the bed to Howe. He quickly kisses his lips and replies, "You could never do anything wrong. I love you just the way you are."

I watch the blush crawl across Howe's cheeks as he nods. "Okay. I suppose a shower is in order, and then cuddles."

Chapter Nine

JANE

I wake surrounded by warmth. Mhm. That's nice; I could get used to this. I snuggle deeper into the heat and then realize in my sleep-ridden state that two bodies are engulfing me. My eyes slowly open to find Alec snuggled close to me with one arm lying over my torso while the other is tucked under his head. His leg is also propped over my own. I look at his face and smile. He looks so peaceful.

I shift just enough to look over my shoulder at Howe. My head is lying on one of his arms, using it as a pillow, and his other arm is wrapped around me and holding onto Alec. The lanterns in my new room provide a soft glow that illuminates Howe's light-chocolate skin perfectly. He looks like a bronze god or something.

Soft piano music floats down the hallway, bringing a smile to my face. Jace! I slowly shimmy out of my cocoon so I don't wake the boys. Once out of the cocoon, I grin as I watch Alec and Howe move into the warm spot I vacated. They wrap their arms around each other, and I hear Alec hum in contentment.

The floor is a bit cold, so I slip on a pair of socks. Slowly, I make my way out the door and down the hallway toward the music. I notice none of the bedrooms have doors, and all are softly lit. I pass what I assume are Alec's and Howe's rooms because they are both empty.

Jace's room is to my right, and as I look to my left, I notice what I assume is Zane's room due to how dark it is compared to the others. I can barely make out the form of a body on the bed. Looking back into Jace's room, I see it's brighter with black and white geometric tiles and black industrial-looking lights hanging from the cave ceiling.

I slowly enter his room and see Jace playing piano in the corner. His eyes are closed, and he's smiling softly. His fingers are graceful as they glide across the piano keys. I instantly recognize the music he's playing. It's one of the few songs he used to play for me as a kid. *River Flows In You*. The version I first heard was from a guy named Yiruma. Jace would have his music on repeat all the time. I used to beg him to play over and over again.

Not wanting to disturb him, I tiptoe to his bed. I situate myself so I'm lying on my belly, watching him play. I close my eyes and enjoy the music as it takes me back to a time I've missed dearly.

"Play it again!" I squeal.

Jace laughs. "You're going to make my fingers fall off if I play anymore, Princess."

"Please. Just one more time, J." I pout.

He sighs. "Fine. But I'm only playing it one more time."

I nod enthusiastically and smile as he plays my favorite song again. Humming along with the music, I close my eyes and lean my head against his shoulder while he plays. "I love this one. It's my favorite," I say with a sigh.

I can hear the smile in Jace's voice when he says, "Considering the number of times I have played this for you, I'm sure you could play it yourself by now. I could download the song for you."

Shaking my head against his shoulder, I say. "I don't want the other version. I want yours."

"Why's that? It sounds exactly the same."

"No, it doesn't. Yours is different."

"How so?" he asks as his fingers glide across the keys.

I shrug. "It just sounds different. It . . . feels different."

He hums. "How does it feel different?"

I smile against his shoulder and reply, "When you play, I feel like it's only you and the guys with me. I don't have to go home. I'm free..."

He's silent for a moment as he plays the last few notes. I'm sad because I don't want to go home once the music ends. He presses the last key but then flows back to the song's beginning again. Leaning his head on mine, he says, "Then I'll play this song for you forever."

The silence surrounding me jerks me out of my memory. I open my eyes to find Jace staring at me from his seat at the piano. He raises a brow in question. "You seemed lost in thought there, Princess."

I smile. "I was lost in a memory."

He hums as he turns back to the piano and starts playing the song again. "Which memory was that?" he asks.

Shifting from my position so that I'm sitting cross-legged on the bed, I answer, "I was remembering when you would play this song for me over and over again."

I see the tilt of his lip as he teases, "Yes, I do remember having to play this so often that my fingers would cramp."

Rolling my eyes, I mumble, "I didn't make you play it that often." He hums but continues playing. I notice that some of the notes don't sound the same as they used to. "Why does the song sound different?"

I see him stiffen, but he doesn't stop playing. He's silent for so long that I don't think he will answer. Then his voice is soft and quiet as he says, "I haven't played this song in over ten years."

Wait, what? I'm taken aback by his words. He hasn't played this song in over ten years? "Why haven't you played it?" I question.

His eyes lift to mine, and I can see his pain in them. "It hurt too much to hear the music," he says quietly.

I stand from the bed and approach the piano before sitting next to him on the bench. "What do you mean?"

His fingers continue to float gracefully across the keys. Now that I'm listening more closely, I can tell that the song isn't the happy one I remember. It now sounds sad. Desperately sad. His eyes are on the keys as he answers, "You weren't there. I couldn't play it without thinking about you. I thought about you EVERY single day, but when I would try to play this song . . ." He pauses and huffs out a sigh. "I could never get farther than a few notes. It was like losing you all over again every time I tried to play this song."

"I'm here now," I whisper. All I can see is his profile, but I can see a sheen in his eyes.

He continues to play, but he's pressing down harder on the keys. Almost like he's desperate to release his emotions, and this is the only way he can. He sucks in a breath as he admits, "I love you. I think I loved you the moment I saw you. But as a kid, you don't really understand love. Over the last ten years, I've realized I always knew you were the one for me."

I stay silent as he continues to play. As I watch, he closes his eyes, and tears slip through his lids to slide down his face. He doesn't stop playing, though. When he speaks again, his voice is rough. "It broke my heart every single time I tried to play this song. I wanted to play it so badly because it was the only thing I had left of you. The only connection I had. But I couldn't play it." He lets out a self-deprecating laugh that sounds wet as he confesses, "I would sit here for hours after trying to play and let every single piece of my heart shatter."

"Jace," I whisper, trying to hold back tears.

He shakes his head. "I remember Zane walking in on me the first time I tried to play it. He sat there with me as I sobbed for what felt like hours. He sat with me every single time after that."

The music fades as he plays the last note. His glassy, dark-brown eyes meet mine, tears still running down his cheeks as he chokes out, "I've loved you for so long, and now you're finally here." He reaches up and cups my cheek. "I'm so afraid, Jane," he whispers.

I put my hand over his. "Why are you afraid?"

"I'm afraid you're not really here. I'm afraid you'll be taken away again. I'm afraid this is just a dream." He closes his eyes and whispers, "I can't do it again, Jane. I can't live through losing you again. My heart won't be able to take it."

Fuck my previous reservations because if I was honest with myself. *Really* honest with myself. I loved him too. I loved all of them. I don't stop myself from pressing my lips softly against his. Our kiss is languid and sweet. There is no rush as we savor this moment. I can taste the saltiness of his tears, but I don't care. Reaching my other hand up, I press it softly over his rapidly beating heart, then tangle my fingers in his shirt and tug him closer.

We kiss until my head spins, and I can no longer breathe. Then I pull away with a soft gasp. I'm panting lightly as I press my forehead to his. His eyes are still closed, but his tears have stopped. "I'm here, Jace. I'm not leaving again." I briefly press my lips against his once more before pulling back to say, "I love you too."

Chapter Ten

JANE

"Let's go, Sephy!" Howe yells as he drags me to the next store. Alec is on my other side, laughing as he drags me by my other arm. It seems even when we go out in the city, I have to go by my alternate name. Now that I'm part of the Underworld, my name has officially changed unless we are completely alone. Seems Howe has already shortened my new name from Persephone to Seph or Sephy.

I laugh as the two of them drag me around. "I'm coming!" I call. Looking behind me briefly, I see a smirk on Jace's and Zane's faces. They are my bodyguards for the day.

Turning forward again, I can't help but giggle as Alec swings around three bags of items I have already purchased. He refused to let me carry them. They are the bright-pink bags you get from Victoria's Secret. Why did we go into Victoria's Secret, you may ask? Well, Howe said that I needed a variety of undergarments and nothing else would do. I didn't argue because what girl doesn't need new, sexy lingerie? Especially now that I'm living with four extremely sexy men.

The guys drag me into a dress store next. Howe releases my hand and claps his together in excitement. He grins over at me as he says, "Alright, Seph. Pick as many dresses as you want. We will split the clothes between the house and the cave, so make sure you pick enough for both."

I can't help but gaze around the store in awe. I have never seen so many fancy dresses in my life. "Why do I need a lot of dresses?"

Alec chimes in, "You will need kick-ass dresses for the meetings. But before we leave, we will stop by another store to get you some casual clothes."

Jace speaks up before I can respond. "Let us spoil you, alright? Pick out as many as you want. Whatever catches your eye."

"We also need to stop by our weapons place to fit her with a few. The store we get our contacts from, too," Zane adds.

Alec pokes me. "Go look around. Pick out whatever you want, and we will put it in a dressing room for you."

Knowing better than to argue, I nod. As I make my way around the store, I find a few dresses I like. There's a dark red two-piece that I really like. It has a deep, sweetheart neckline that will make my boobs look great. The back has several crisscrossed pieces of fabric, and the bottom is a floor-length, flowy chiffon. I immediately reach out to find my size.

"I've got it. Keep looking," Howe tells me as he shifts through the dresses.

I roll my eyes but do as I'm told. As I walk through the store, I realize that the ones I like are dresses I wouldn't normally wear. But Persephone? Persephone is the Queen of the Underworld. And she likes to wear things that make her feel sexy. I find another dress that's black with small flowers all over. But this dress has a high slit up one side, and the lower part is made up of several layers of sheer material. The top is a corset with boning. It has beaded flowers and is completely sheer except for the top half.

I point to it, knowing that Howe is right behind me. He lets out an appreciative hum, and I can't help but smile. Noticing a more risque section, I head in that direction. I can't help but squeal when I see the next two dresses. One is a deep red, so dark it's almost black. It has a sheer, off-the-shoulder top with intricate flowers sewn into it that would cover my cleavage. The bottom looks like a pair of underwear, but two deep-red pieces of fabric are attached. One attaches to the side of the hip and wraps around the back to attach to the other hip. Then there's a bunched piece of fabric in the front, giving the illusion that there are two high slits in the dress.

The second dress is black and has a see-through-lace bodice with intricate straps flowing over the front and onto the back of the dress. The bottom is the same concept as the first, except the fabric is see-through.

Knowing Howe has grabbed the dresses I like, I head to the changing area but stop when I notice Howe at the register paying with a bag in his hand. Heading his way, I say, "I thought I was going to try everything on?"

He shakes his head. "I already know these are going to look great. No need to try them on."

A grunt behind me has me looking over my shoulder. Alec is walking toward us, holding several shoe boxes. He has them stacked up and is holding them under his chin. I think he's managing about six boxes. Impressive. "Do you need help?" I ask.

"Nope. I've got everything under control." He slides the boxes onto the counter without dropping a single one. Doubly impressed.

"What are all the shoes for?"

He grins at me and says, "For you, silly."

"I don't need that many shoes, Al . . . Charon." Fuck, I almost slipped up and called him his real name in public.

He lets out a laugh as he pays for the shoes. "Seph, these are only your heels. We still need to get you some normal shoes and some boots."

My eyes widen. "I really don't need that many shoes."

Jace's dark voice comes from behind me. "Let them spoil you, Princess."

I growl because I know I'm going to cave. I love shoes. "Fine," I say with a groan.

"We should also grab her some leathers for when we go out. She can't wear dresses out in public and be able to fight if she needs to," Zane adds.

Jace nods. "Agreed. Do you think the guy we get ours from would be able to make a special order for her?"

Zane shrugs. "I can't see why not."

"So where are we going?" I ask with a sigh.

Howe and Alec each slide a hand into one of mine and smile as they pull me out of the store. "You'll see," Alec teases while laughing. I shrug. I'm just going to go along with whatever they have planned for the day.

We are walking down the sidewalk when a woman stops and stares at Howe and Alec. She just stands there staring. I watch as she looks them up and down before smiling and shifting her upper body to make her breasts look larger.

For the record, I'm not proud of what I do next. The woman looks right at me and smirks as she makes her way over to us. Without thinking, I lift and lick both Howe's and Alec's hands. Surprisingly, that doesn't deter her. So . . . I turn and tug Howe down to kiss him forcefully on the lips. He growls when I turn and does the exact same thing to Alec. When I turn back around, I find the woman staring wide-eyed at me.

I give her a maniacal grin and growl out, "Mine!"

The woman immediately turns and runs in the opposite direction. I can't help but stand a little taller. Howe and Alec both bust out in laughter.

"Did you seriously just lick us?" Alec asks through his laughter.

Howe snorts and says, "Did you see that chick? She was fucking freaked. She ran so fast."

With a shrug, I continue walking. "Bitch knew you were with me."

"Did she now?" Alec teases.

"Yes," I huff out.

"Seems we have a possessive Queen," Jace says behind me.

I hum as I reply, "You are the one who said you all are mine."

"She does have a point, Hades," Zane agrees.

Grinning over my shoulder, I say, "You did say you loved me, right, Hades?"

He stiffens briefly before answering, "That I did, my Persephone."

I wink at him before turning back around. I keep walking. "Then the women around here need to realize that you are mine."

Howe bumps my shoulder. "He said he loved you?"

I hum. "He did."

"Did you say it back?" Alec asks beside me.

I nod. "I did."

Howe tugs on my hand, so I turn to look at him. His brows are pinched, and I can't tell what he's thinking, but after a moment, he says, "I love you, Persephone."

I tug him toward me until his face is in front of mine, then I kiss the tip of his nose. "I love you too."

His eyes widen, and then a huge smile spreads across his face. He kisses the tip of my nose before straightening. With a grin, he says, "You're stuck with this dog now, Seph."

I laugh. "I wouldn't want it any other way, Cerby."

Alec tugs on my hand, so I turn to look at him. His cheeks are slightly pink as he says softly, "I love you."

"Love you too," I say back before tugging him down to kiss his cheek.

He smirks as we continue walking down the street. I can't help but look over my shoulder and see Zane watching us. His eyes meet mine as I mouth, "I love you."

I see the tilt of his lips as he mouths back, "I love you too."

Giving him a beaming smile, I continue down the sidewalk as my boys drag me to more stores. I know that this kind of happiness won't last long; it never does, so I'm going to soak up every moment before the other shoe drops and life shits on me again.

Chapter Eleven

JANE

"So when do I get my Persephone tattoos?" I ask, mainly out of curiosity. We are all hanging out in my bedroom at the compound until we leave for the house later. The guys wanted to drop off some of the clothes here first.

Jace looks up from his paperwork. He's currently sitting on the floor, leaning up against the side of the bed. "What do you mean?" he asks.

I point toward his face and say, "You all have face tattoos to go with your names. When do I get mine?"

He raises a brow in surprise. "You want a face tattoo?"

I shrug. "Why not. You all look pretty badass. And you have to admit that with the pink UV contacts I got, having a face tattoo would look awesome."

He smirks and turns back to his paperwork. "Face tattoos hurt. How about we stick to UV face paint for now, Princess?"

I huff out a sigh. "Fine. What about my other tattoos?"

"What other tattoos?" Zane asks from his spot on the floor. He's currently lying down with a hand over his face.

"You know. My Persephone-inspired tattoos."

Zane lifts his arm from his face to squint up at me. "What are you talking about?"

I point toward his hands. "You have skeletal tattoos on your hands. I have a hard time believing that you don't have any Thanatos-inspired tattoos on you."

He sighs and lowers his arm back over his face with a shrug. "Maybe I do."

"Can I see?" I ask in excitement.

He lifts his arm again. "Seriously?"

I roll my eyes. "Duh! Of course, I'm serious! I got to see Alec's and Howe's in the shower, but I know you and Jace have tattoos, too. I want to see!" Alec and Howe each have several tattoos, but their code name tats are easy to spot.

Alec has an obol coin on each hand. The front of the coin is inked on the top of his right hand, with the back on top of his left hand. He had explained that lore said the obol coin was a form of payment for the Ferryman. He also has a large tattoo of the Ferryman on his back. I have to admit; it looks dark and scary.

Howe has a large tattoo of Cerberus on his back. The three-headed dog has large fangs and drooling maws. They are poised as if ready to attack their enemies. The tattoo on his chest is a serpent winding through a skull. I had asked how that had anything to do with his name, but he just said, "I am Hades' dog of war. I will fight to protect my family."

Zane huffs out a sigh and sits up. He pushes himself up off the floor and pulls his shirt over his head, revealing his deliciously-toned body. I have to bite my lip to make sure my mouth doesn't drop open, and I don't start drooling. The first thing I notice isn't the tattoo on his chest, though. No, my eyes are drawn to his black nipple bars with spikes on either end. Well damn! That's sexy as fuck. Shaking myself, I focus on the art on his chest. It's a black and white tattoo that looks like a butterfly, but there's an outline of a skull within its body. He turns around, and I see that he has the typical symbol of death on his back. It's a cloaked figure with a curved scythe.

I hum in approval. "Beautiful."

He grunts as he pulls his shirt back down and resumes his position on the floor. "Should be considering how much the fucker cost," he grumbles.

I look over at Jace and raise a brow. He returns the look. Rolling my eyes, I say, "Your turn."

He rolls his eyes in response as if I'm exhausting but grins. Setting his paperwork beside him, he stands from the floor. He turns, giving me a wink, before doing one of those sexy, one-armed moves that have women everywhere drooling. You know the move I'm talking about. The one where the guy takes off his shirt using one arm and looks sexy as fuck doing it.

I gasp in surprise when I see just how much of his skin is covered in tattoos. On his chest is a large screech owl with its wings spread wide. The detail in the linework and shading makes the owl look like it's about to fly right off his skin.

Jace twists his forearm to reveal a snake wrapped in a figure eight with its jaws open wide. Where the snake's tail would normally be, there is a skull. That's when I realize the snake is coming out of the skull's open jaw. He turns his other forearm, and on it, I see the scepter of Hades.

He turns around so I can see the large Hades piece on his back. It's of a bearded male wearing a skull on the top of his head like a headdress. There are cypress leaves surrounding the male as well.

Well damn. All my males are tatted up. Hum . . . I wonder. Jace seems to have the most tattoos and piercings out of all my guys. Putting his shirt back on, he turns around.

"How many piercings do you have?" I ask.

He raises a brow but answers, "Seven."

I try to remember the piercings I've seen so far. He has one in his eyebrow and one in his ear that are easy to spot, but where are the others? "I've only seen two."

He sticks his tongue out so I can see a black barbell with a skull on top of it. But I'm still confused. That only makes three.

"That's only three."

He smirks and briefly looks down at his crotch. When he looks back up, he gives me a wink and turns back to his paperwork.

I choke on my spit. He has four piercings on his dick!? Well, fuck, now I'm all hot and bothered. And SEVERELY intrigued. I turn to Zane, trying to distract myself. "How many piercings do you have, Thanatos?"

He holds up three fingers. So those would be his snake bite and both nipples. From my spot on the bed, I shout, "How many piercings do you have, Charon?"

When we got home, Alec and Howe decided to put my stuff away. Considering the amount of shit they bought, it doesn't surprise me that it's taking so long. Alec pops out of the bathroom with a bag of bath salts and says, "I have three. You should know that." He laughs as he pops back into the bathroom.

"Just wanted to make sure I didn't miss any."

Before I can ask Howe, I hear him yell, "I don't have any piercings, Seph."

"How are things going in there?" I call back, changing the subject.

"Almost finished," Alec hollers.

With a shrug, I fall back onto the bed. I can't stop myself from snuggling into the blankets. Patting the bed next to me, I say, "Come snuggle with me, Thanatos. I'm sure it's more comfortable up here than on the ground."

"I'm not really a snuggler," he replies from his spot on the floor.

I laugh. "Just come up here and snuggle with me, you fucker."

He snorts, then grunts as he gets up. I feel him fall onto the bed beside me and grin. I snuggle closer to him, and he wraps an arm around me. "Better, Persephone?"

I hum in contentment as I close my eyes. "Much better." We lie in silence for a few minutes before I whisper, "I love you."

Zane's arms tighten around me as he pulls me closer. I feel his lips press softly against the top of my head as he whispers back, "I love you too."

Chapter Twelve

JANE

We seem to be driving to the middle of nowhere. And when I say nowhere, I mean NOWHERE. America never really recovered from the wars over half a century ago. But people often forget history, and it ends up repeating itself. Although let's be honest, the government wanted everyone to forget our history, and sadly they did. Me? I know what the fuck happened. The government got greedy like they always do, and the American people were too blind to realize that no one in high society gave a flying fuck about the little guys. Unless they got publicity for it.

So, by the time the people realized they couldn't protect themselves, the three major powers of the World had decided that they wanted to see who was number one. Spoiler alert, there was no winner in that fight. Lands were destroyed, and in an effort to fix what they had done, the government rearranged the territories. The United States of America is gone, and in its place is just America. It's been fifty years, and I've got to say . . . the people in power still don't give a fuck. That's why my boys are trying to make a difference.

We turn onto a road with a large gate in front, and I gasp. I look out the windows on either side of the car, and it looks like the gate goes on forever. Jace pulls up to it and puts in a code. The large black gate opens, and we continue down a long driveway.

I start bouncing in my seat when the house comes into view. Can it be considered a house if it's a three-story mansion? "Holy shit! Is this your house?!"

Jace laughs softly from the front and says, "This is OUR house. We have Hellhounds who guard the perimeter when we stay here. There's a guest house outside the gate where they can stay in shifts."

Once the car is parked, I crawl over Howe's lap and open the door. I almost fall to the ground in my haste but manage to catch myself.

Howe laughs at me. "Slow down, Starlight. The house isn't going any-where."

Jumping up and down, I yell, "Let's go. Let's Go!" I run up to the front door as the guys follow, laughing at my excitement. The last time I was in a house this big, it was my dad's place. I can't wait to see what they did with this big house.

Jace opens the front door for me, and I rush inside. Wow. I don't know how else to describe it other than grand. "This . . . this is amazing."

Howe comes up beside me and tugs on my hand. "We can give you the full tour later; let's show you your room." He drags me behind him as we walk up the extremely grand stairs.

"How did you end up with this big of a place?" I ask, staring around in awe as he drags me down a hallway.

Zane speaks up, and I jump a bit, not having realized everyone is follow-ing. "We bought this place at a severe discount. The house was run down and needed a lot of updates."

"We thought that we needed a place away from the cave. A place where we can relax and just be ourselves," Jace adds.

I snort. "This seems like a lot of room just for relaxing."

Alec walks up next to me and smiles. "We also have a shooting range out back and a large gym in the basement."

Howe hums. "And a huge kitchen."

I laugh and ask, "Who cooks?"

Looking over my shoulder, I see Alec and Howe point behind them while Jace points at Zane with a grin. "He's the best cook around here."

Zane grunts. "I had to learn how to cook. Every single one of you idiots burned everything, and I'm pretty sure Alec burned boiling water."

"How do you burn boiling water?" I ask; I didn't even know that was possible.

Zane shrugs. "I have no idea, but none of them are allowed in the kitchen to cook anymore. We went through five sets of pots and pans before they realized they should leave everything up to me.

Howe rubs the back of his head. "I wanted to make sure I couldn't learn how to cook."

Zane shakes his head. "Well, you can't."

I bump Howe's shoulder and say, "It's okay. I can't cook worth shit either."

He grins at me, then opens the door to my new room. "Good to know. Welcome home, Jane."

I can't help but smile as I look around. It looks like an exact replica of the bedroom I have in the cave. The only difference is the walls here are painted, whereas the cave has rock walls. The ceiling is black, and the walls are off-white, making the red in the room pop.

I can't help but run over and jump onto the bed belly first. I bounce, then snuggle into the blankets, humming in approval. "How are these so soft and fluffy?"

Alec laughs as he slides in next to me on the bed. "We found this store that has the best bedsheets and blankets. We haven't gone anywhere else since."

Closing my eyes, I snuggle deeper into the blankets and sigh.

"Do you want to take a nap, Princess?" Jace asks from the edge of the bed.

I hum and say, "Only if you snuggle with me."

Jace laughs. I hear the shuffling of shoes, then feel his body slide in next to mine. I open my eyes when I feel Alec pull away. "You don't have to leave."

He smiles and presses a kiss on my forehead. "Howe and I are going to work on putting your stuff away while Zane starts dinner. Enjoy your cuddles, Moonbeam."

Once the others have left, I flip onto my side and look at Jace. Zane dimmed the lights, so it's dark, but I can still make out Jace's face. He stares at me, and after a few minutes of this, I can't help but ask, "Why are you staring at me?"

His smile is soft as he lifts a hand and brushes his fingers softly across my cheeks. "I'm not staring. I'm admiring."

A grin pulls at my lips. "There's a difference?"

He bends forward and kisses my nose before pulling away. "Staring makes me sound creepy and like a stalker."

"And admiring?"

Cupping my cheek gently, he says, "Memorizing every single thing about you so I never forget."

"I'm not sure if that sounds any better," I tease.

His lips tilt into a smile. "Would it sound better if I said I did it out of love? And because of how much I missed you."

I snuggle closer to him with a sleepy smile. "Maybe," I whisper.

He wraps his arms around me and pulls me into his body, holding me close as he whispers, "I love you, and I missed you."

I hum and take in a deep breath of his woodsy smell. I feel myself relaxing as I'm engulfed in his warmth and smell. It's not long before I fall into the darkness and dream of my boys.

Chapter Thirteen

ZANE

10 years ago...

I'm wiping her face as gently as I can, but I'm not the gentle one. That's Alec and sometimes Howe depending on the day. But me? I'm the big kid who solves more problems with his fists rather than providing a healing touch. She winces again as I touch a sensitive spot on her cheek. "Sorry, Sunshine."

She grins at me as I continue wiping the dirt and blood off her face. "Why are you sorry? You're not the one who smacked me."

I stiffen, trying not to growl at her words. No, I wasn't. Her father was the one who smacked her and left her in the mud. Luckily, we were in the tree house and saw it go down. The others shoved her at me to clean up while they kept a lookout for her dad.

She stops my hand with hers as she holds onto my wrist. My eyes meet her gray-blue ones. They are filled with so much strength—too much for a ten-year-old to need. She gives me a crooked smile. "Don't be such a grouch, Z. It's okay. It doesn't hurt that bad."

I frown. "You have been wincing the whole time I've been cleaning your face."

She just rolls her eyes at me in typical Jane fashion. "Okay, maybe it hurts a little. But you're not the one who did this, so stop acting like you're causing the pain."

I lower my eyes and quietly say, "I am hurting you."

She slips her tiny fingers under my chin and lifts my face to meet her gaze. Smiling sadly, she protests, "You would never hurt me, Z. You protect me more than anyone." She giggles. "My own personal bodyguard."

"I didn't protect you this time," I whisper.

"You can't ALWAYS protect me, Zane. I'm stuck with my dad for a while. But one day, we will get away."

I continue wiping the dirt from her face. "I promised I would protect you," I say, feeling a bit lost.

She boops me on the nose and smiles despite the fact that her face must hurt. "And you do."

I growl at her insistence. "Fine. One day we will get you far away from that fucker."

She nods as she says with a smile, "I know."

A week later...

Jace jumps down from the tree house, and I follow. I heard the yelling and screaming. What the fuck is happening? I watch as Jace runs toward a struggling Jane. Her father is dragging her out of the house. I start running toward them when I'm suddenly grunting against the ground. Looking up, I find a large, masked guy on top of me.

I punch and kick, trying to get this guy off me, but it isn't making any difference because of my size. I may be big, but I'm still just a kid. The guy holding me down is a full-grown adult. He grunts when I land a solid punch to his cheek but doesn't let go of me.

He yells something, and suddenly, there's another masked figure on top of me. I scream and fight as hard as I can. Fuck! I'm getting tired when all of a sudden, the weight holding me down is gone. I sit up, quickly looking around.

"Where the fuck did they go?" I ask quietly.

"I don't know, but . . ."

Hearing Howe's voice, I look over to find him staring behind me, eyes wide. I twist to see Jace standing quietly, his fists clenching and unclenching. Looking around again, I take in everything. That's when it clicks. Where's Jane?

"Where's Jane?" I ask, but it seems like no one hears me. I jump up off the ground and run over to Jace. I'm standing beside him when I look in the direction he's staring. I don't see anything, so I look back to our leader. My eyes widen when I see tears sliding down his face. Jace never cries. I haven't seen my brother cry in all the years I've been with him. He's the strongest guy I know.

I continue watching as he reaches up and rubs his chest, grimacing. Shifting so that my side brushes up against his, I ask quietly, "What are we going to do?"

Jace looks over at me with sad eyes. He looks so lost. So broken. Turning, he stares back in the direction I assume Jane was taken. He remains silent, not answering my question. I can't do anything but stare in the same direction as my brothers.

I promised that I would protect her. I failed. I promised that we would take her away from her father. I failed at that too. I've failed my Sunshine. There's a sudden searing pain in my chest, and I reach up to rub at the spot. Fuck, that hurts.

Right here, right now, I make a silent vow that when I find my Sunshine, I will protect her no matter what. I will protect her at any cost.

Chapter Fourteen

JANE

Present Day...

"Alright, we need to head to the cave for a few meetings today," Jace says as he grabs his to-go mug off the kitchen counter.

I point to the mug. "Coffee?"

He raises a brow. "Do I look like someone who would drink coffee?"

Rolling my eyes, I reply, "No, I guess not. Tea?"

He smirks. "Of course, it's tea."

I let out a groan of exasperation. "Please tell me someone in this fucking house drinks coffee. I will die if I have to drink dirty plant water."

"It's tea, not plant water," Jace defends.

Putting my hand on my hip, I pop it out with attitude. I point to his mug and gripe, "It's a bunch of plants in hot-ass water."

He arches a brow again. "That would make your coffee, bean water."

I shrug but don't disagree. "It's fucking delicious bean water."

"Okay, okay, kids." Alec laughs and hands me a mug. "I drink coffee, don't worry. Here is your mug."

Taking a sip, I groan loudly. Fuck yeah. Chocolatey, sugary caffeine! "I fucking love you!"

"Love you too," Alec responds with a grin.

I point to my coffee. "I was talking to the coffee." I laugh at his frown but follow up with, "But I love you too, Alec."

He rolls his eyes as if he's used to my antics. I guess, in some ways, I haven't changed all that much. "Let's go, troublemaker."

Howe bounces over and kisses my cheek. "Do I get an I love you too, or did Alec and the coffee take all the love?" he teases.

I giggle and give him a quick kiss on the lips. "I love you, Howe!"

He grins. "Love you too, Starlight."

"Alright, now that everyone has gotten some love. Can we leave, please?" Jace asks from the front door while gesturing out the door. "Let's go."

I laugh as I make my way past him, bouncing up onto my tiptoes to kiss him on the cheek. "Oh, don't get sour. I love you too, J."

He rolls his eyes, but I can see the smirk he tries to hide as he locks the door behind us. I can't stop grinning as we make our way to the car. It's been so long since I've laughed or even smiled this much.

The drive is a lot faster than I remembered it being last night. We park in front of the cave, and I start to get out of the car, but Howe holds my arm to stop me. I raise a brow in question.

"Let the others out first."

I'm confused by his tone, but I shrug it off. Jace is already by the cave entrance, but he's looking around as if waiting for something to happen. Howe and Alec exit the car from the other side. Zane opens the door for me, but he's acting more like a shield rather than opening my door just to be nice.

"What's going—" Before I finish my question, shots ring out around us. Zane covers my body with his, and I feel him jerk. Did he just get shot?!

I hear Jace scream, "Shots fired! Alpha and Beta to my location immediately!"

I'm stuck under Zane, so I try to push him off of me to get a look at what's going on. He growls and orders, "Sit fucking still till we get backup!"

Freaking the fuck out, I do as I'm told. There's a sudden increase of shots fired, then Jace yells, "Get her the fuck inside, Thanatos!"

Zane doesn't hesitate. He picks me up and runs to the entrance of the cave. The others soon follow, and I'm hyperventilating as my gaze darts around. I take in my boys and notice they have holes in their clothes. Fuck, they've been shot! Heart pounding in fear, I race over to Jace first and finger the holes in his shirt, expecting blood to be seeping out of them. But . . . there's nothing. I rip his shirt off and realize he is wearing a bulletproof vest.

As I look around at my other guys, my brain slowly starts coming out of the adrenaline haze. Then it clicks. They are all wearing vests. Except me. That's why I wasn't allowed out of the car without them. Then my anger sparks. They could have fucking died trying to protect me, and instead of explaining the danger of whatever the fuck just happened and putting a vest on me . . . they didn't!

I notice Alpha and Beta looking at me, each with a raised brow, so I give them a forced smile and say, "Thank you for the backup." I then look at my guys and give them a death glare that could rival any death glare. I'm sure I make Persephone proud when I growl out, "My room. NOW!"

"Now, Persephone . . ." Jace starts, but when my eyes snap to him, his eyes widen, and he immediately shuts up.

"You wanted a Queen. Get your fucking asses to my bedroom now!"

"Um . . . we'll start a perimeter search." Alpha clears his throat, bows to us, and runs out of the room.

Beta shakes his head with a smirk of amusement. "You've fucked yourselves now." Jace glares at the guy, but it only makes him laugh as he slowly backs away. "No offense, Hades." He points to me, saying, "The Queen is always scarier." He bows to me before turning and running after Alpha.

The guys sigh as they nod and make their way to my bedroom. By the time we get to my room, I am seething. Why the fuck didn't they give me a bulletproof vest? No, without even talking to me, they just decided that if I needed protecting, they would take the bullet for me.

The guys watch as I pace the bedroom, and I know they can tell I'm pissed. I'm pretty sure I made that clear when I ordered them to my room. But right now, I can only deal with the guy who pissed me off the most. I'll deal with the others when I yell at them for the lack of communication. I turn to glare at them. "Everyone, get the fuck out!" I point at Zane as I say with a growl, "Except for you."

The guys look at each other, then Howe shrugs and says, "Good luck, bro." Howe pats Zane on the shoulder as he leaves. The others give Zane a sympathetic look before they follow behind.

I continue my pacing, trying to ground myself so I don't try to rip his head off. I don't know if that's possible, but I'm sure I could make it happen somehow. Zane sighs and asks, "Why are you so pissed? I saved your life, Seph."

I turn and give him the nastiest glare I possibly can. I'm not sure if it comes across as a glare, but I'm going with it. I point at him. "That isn't the fucking point." I growl.

He throws his hands in the air. "Then what's the fucking point?!"

I'm seething as I reply, "You could have told me what was going on! You could have given me a bulletproof vest! I'm the fucking Queen of this Underworld now, am I not?!"

"Yes," He growls.

"Then you guys should have told me shit was going down! I'm not a fucking idiot! I know you guys have enemies, but if I need to be prepared, you have to fucking tell me that shit. Do you understand?!" I feel like I'm screaming; I probably am.

"Yes, My Queen," he forces out.

"I don't want you to EVER fucking do that again. You are not my fucking bulletproof shield! Do you understand?"

He grunts and says, "I'm not going to promise that. I'll always protect you, no matter what."

I stomp over till I'm standing in front of him. Rising on my tiptoes, I yell, "You won't be protecting me if you're fucking dead!"

His eyes blaze with fire as he responds in a low voice. "Then I'll die a fucking happy man knowing you're alive."

I slap him across the face. "How fucking dare you."

He grabs my hand as I go to slap him again, and my vision blurs. I scream, "How fucking dare you!"

"I won't fail to protect you again. Not again. Do you hear me?" he whispers, his voice cracking at the end.

I look up at his face, ready to scream at him again when I see tears in his eyes. He cups my cheek lovingly and wipes away my tears. I didn't even realize I was crying. Resting his forehead against mine, he grits his teeth and says, "I can't fail again. I wouldn't survive losing you a second time."

Chapter Fifteen

ZANE

Thirty minutes ago...

Thankfully, I'm on the side that the door blocks my blind side as I help Jane out of the car. I'm not completely blind out of my left eye, but people take advantage of blind spots. I catch a glint out of the corner of my good eye, and out of instinct, I automatically cover her body with mine. IA shot rings out, and I grunt. FUCKING HELL! Motherfucker, that shit hurts. Yeah, I have a bulletproof vest on, but that shit still hurts. Anyone who tells you otherwise is a lying bitch. I grunt again as another bullet hits me in the back. Those are going to bruise like a bitch.

Jane is shaking from the barrage of gunfire going on around us. I hear Jace shouting orders, but I stay where I am until I hear my name. Jane starts wiggling underneath me, and I growl, "Sit fucking still till we get backup." Like a good girl, she listens. Bout fucking time. I can see the defiance in her eyes when Jace gives her an order. She doesn't follow because she has to; she follows because she wants to make Jace happy. For now.

Jace yells my name, and I listen for my orders. When he tells me to move, I immediately pick Jane up and run to the cave entrance. Once inside, I set her down and try to catch my breath. As the others make their way toward us, I step away. Jane looks around at each of us, breathing hard. She races over to Jace after noticing holes in his shirt. She fingers the holes for a second and then rips his shirt off.

I see the moment it clicks for her as she looks around at each of us. We outfitted ourselves with bulletproof vests but didn't give her one. We haven't discussed what is going on in our world with her yet. There's a fire in her eyes when she looks at each of us. Standing before us now isn't the Jane we know. Right now, she's Persephone. The Queen of the Underworld.

She murmurs something to Alpha and Beta before turning to us. "My room. NOW," she commands. I have to suppress a shiver when her voice sounds like that.

Jace starts to argue with her, but the moment her eyes meet his, his body stiffens, and he instantly shuts up. Looks like the almighty Hades won't go against our Queen either. Not when she fired up like this.

She stands taller as she yells, "You wanted a Queen. Get your fucking asses to my bedroom now!"

Alpha and Beta say their goodbyes, and we do as we're told, making our way to her bedroom. The moment we get inside, she starts pacing back and forth. I can see the fire inside her building. I know she's pissed at us. Pissed at me most of all, but I don't regret what I did for a moment.

I didn't even realize I was looking at the ground until I hear her commanding voice again. She's pointing at me when she orders, "Except for you."

Howe pats me on the shoulder as they leave. The others give me a sympathetic look. They know I'm fucked. I know I'm fucked. Once everyone is gone, I let out a deep sigh and ask, "Why are you so pissed? I saved your life, Seph."

I have to admit, the glare she sends me makes my balls shrivel up. Fuck, I'm glad she doesn't have any weapons. I'm pretty sure she would unalive me right now. She points a finger at me as she growls. "That's not the fucking point!"

Unable to control my own emotions at the moment, I throw my hands in the air. "Then what's the fucking point?!"

She's seething as she spits out, "You could have told me what was going on! You could have given me a bulletproof vest! I'm the fucking Queen of this Underworld now, am I not?!"

She's right; we should have told her what was going on. We should have given her a vest to protect herself. She is the Queen of the Underworld. She's our Queen, which is why we wanted to protect her from our world as long as we could. "Yes," I growl.

"Then you guys should have told me shit was going down! I'm not a fucking idiot! I know you guys have enemies, but if I need to be prepared, you have to fucking tell me that shit. Do you understand?!" She's screaming at this point, and I have to stop myself from wincing at how high-pitched her voice is.

I take a deep breath and force out, "Yes, My Queen."

"I don't want you to EVER fucking do that again. You are not my fucking bulletproof shield! Do you understand?"

Shaking my head, I grunt and reply, "I'm not going to promise that; I'll protect you no matter what."

She stomps over, stopping in front of me and standing on her tiptoes as she yells, "You won't be protecting me if you're fucking dead!"

I can feel the tight grip I have on my emotions slipping. Every single emotion I've held back for the last ten years is slipping through my fingers. I growl out, "Then I'll die a fucking happy man knowing you're alive."

She slaps me across the face. "How fucking dare you," she says, still seething.

I'm surprised by the slap, but as she goes to do it again, I grab her hand. I can see tears gathering in her eyes as she screams, "How fucking dare you!"

My chest tightens, and the titanium wall I spent years building around my heart shatters in that moment. "I won't fail to protect you again. Not again, Do you hear me?" I whisper.

Her eyes meet mine, and she opens her mouth to scream at me again, but something stops her. I cup her face and gently wipe away her tears. My vision starts to blur as I rest my forehead against hers. "I can't fail again. I wouldn't survive losing you a second time."

I've failed her for so long. I failed to take her away from her father. I failed to protect her when she was ten, and she was ripped away from us. I failed to find her these last ten years, and because of that, I failed to protect her. I can't fail her again. Not when my Sunshine, my light, has finally come back to us.

Jace and I have lived in the dark since she was stolen from us. We did our best to put up a strong front for Howe and Alec. When Jace broke that day he tried to play their song, I made sure Howe and Alec were gone. I stayed beside him every time he tried to play. We broke together. After each attempt, we would gather our shattered pieces and put on a brave face regardless of how broken we were.

But right now, I can't do it. I can't fake it. "I've failed you for so long, Sunshine," I choke out.

She reaches up to cup my face, her small, delicate fingers stroking my cheeks. I close my eyes and feel myself shatter at her touch. The tears I've held back for ten years begin to fall in earnest. I release my grip on her face as she pulls me down, shoving my face into her neck. She wraps her arms around my neck and holds me tight.

"You haven't failed me, Z," she whispers, barely loud enough for me to hear.

I wrap my arms around her and hold her as close as possible. I need to feel that she's real and here with me. My body trembles as I try to suck in a breath in an attempt to hold back the sobs wanting to take control. "I can't lose my Sunshine. I need to protect you. I CAN'T fail again." My voice cracks at the end.

She slips her fingers into my hair, gently scratching my scalp. "I'm here. I'm safe. You protected me. But you guys need to tell me these things. I've protected myself for the last ten years. You can protect me, but I need to protect you too."

I pick her up and carry her over to the bed, then sit so she's straddling my lap. Pulling her close, I rest my face in the crook of her neck again. I take a deep inhale of her lilac scent. It calms my thumping heart, the burn behind my eyes subsiding. As we lie together, I remember the song I used to whisper to her ever so often when she had a horrible day with her dad. She would cuddle close, even then.

I hold her tighter as I remember part of the lyrics. I pull away just far enough so she can hear my whispered words, "Please . . . please don't take my Sunshine away."

Chapter Sixteen

JANE

We sat there wrapped in each other for what felt like hours but was really only a few minutes. Eventually, Zane sighs and pulls away. "We need to get ready for the meeting. Do you need help with your skull makeup?" he asks.

I shake my head. "I should be fine. I'll meet you guys down there." I press my lips against his briefly before sliding off his lap. He groans, and I can't help but laugh. He eyes me for a moment as if debating whether or not he should leave me. I smile as I make my way to the bathroom. "Go get ready," I say over my shoulder.

He hums. "Fine. I'll send Alpha and Beta to walk you down." I listen for the door to close behind him, and I laugh because that door wasn't there the other day. I hadn't noticed it in my anger, but it seems they don't want a Hellhound to walk by and see something they aren't supposed to.

I walk into my closet and look around. What do I want to wear on my first official day as Persephone? I feel like I should wear black, and I can pair my outfit with my dark pink crown the guys got me. Searching through the dresses, I find the black sheer-lace dress with straps. I know I need to get the dress on before I do my makeup.

Slipping into the dress, I look in the mirror. My mouth drops because I look nothing like myself. Shaking myself, I grab one of the boxes of heels Alec bought. I open the first box and instantly decide I'm wearing them. They have a tall black heel that is maybe three inches high. They look like snake scales, and instead of a strap around my ankle, there is a golden snake. I grin because it goes with Jace's persona of Hades.

I place them on the bathroom counter to slip them on when I'm done. Finding my pink UV contacts, I put them in before starting my makeup. I am not one of those girls who can put contacts in with a face full of makeup. I make my eyes dark and pair it with a deep red lip stain. As the finishing touch, I put the dark pink crown on, and I must admit, I look badass.

With a deep sigh, I know it's time to do my skull makeup. I regret telling Zane that I didn't need any help, but it's too late now. I grab my pink UV paint and a small paintbrush, ready to get to work. Each time I make a mistake, I growl. When I make a mistake yet again, I scream.

There's a knock at my door before I hear, "Are you alright, Miss?"

I groan. Fuck. I walk to the door to my room and open it but wince and apologize when I see who's there. "Sorry, Alpha, Beta. I just . . . I keep fucking up my skull makeup."

Now that I have a better look, I can see they look like brothers. I watch as they look at each other, then Alpha sighs and nods to Beta. Beta smiles and offers, "I can help if you'd like?"

"Really?"

He nods. "Yep. It seems we are your personal bodyguards while you are at the compound."

"Don't you guys have other jobs more important than guarding me? I'm sure one of the other Hellhounds could protect me."

Alpha shakes his head. "Hades doesn't trust anyone other than us with your protection."

I arch a brow. "He doesn't trust any of his other men?"

Beta pipes in as he slides into the room, heading to my bathroom. "He doesn't trust anyone other than us with your safety."

"And why does he trust you?" I ask as I follow behind him.

He smirks over his shoulder. "Because we have proven our loyalty."

I hum in response. Not much I could ask to follow up that answer. He points to the counter and says, "Up you go."

I hop onto the counter, noticing Alpha followed us. Now that they don't have their contacts in, I can see their normal eye color. They both have hazel-brown eyes with swirls of green. I look between the two of them and can't help but ask, "Are you two brothers?"

Alpha grunts. "Yes, Miss."

I grin. "I'm going to have to come up with a different name for you guys. I know I can't call you by your real names, but I can't keep calling you Alpha and Beta. It doesn't sound right."

Beta has a soft smile as he lifts the brush and starts painting my face. "You seem interested in us for someone who is supposed to be our boss."

I roll my eyes. "I'm not really your boss. Hades is."

"You are Persephone. You are part of the rulers of the Underworld. Therefore, you are our boss," Alpha says.

I think about that for a moment. He's right, but . . . I don't want to be a boss. I have my boys back, but I don't have anyone else. My eyes roam over the man in front of me. Is it hard for them to keep their work and personal lives separate? "Why did you decide to work for Hades?"

They both stiffen at my question, and I immediately start to backpedal. "You don't have to answer. I was just curious." It's quiet for a moment before Alpha speaks.

"Our father was one of the politicians Hades took down. Hades saw potential in us. We weren't polluted by greed like our father was. We helped Hades take over the territory, and in thanks, we run the Underground when we aren't working with him."

I look between the two of them and recognition clicks. They changed their looks just enough, so you wouldn't know who they were unless you really looked. You wouldn't see the resemblance if they had their contacts in and all the gear they normally wear on. But I've learned to watch people over the years. I memorized every face that looked important in case they had connections to my father.

"You're the Steepe brothers," I whisper quietly. The brush pauses on my face, and I look between them to see their eyes widen. I shrug. "I memorized the faces of everyone who held power. I didn't want to run into anyone of importance who knew my father."

They exchange a brief glance before nodding, confirming my words. I know who they are now, but that comes with knowing there are supposed to be four of them. "I'm sorry for your loss," I whisper.

I see Alpha clench his jaw before nodding with a curt, "Thank you."

In an attempt to lighten the mood, I say, "So I need to come up with nicknames for you two now."

Beta continues painting swirls on my face as he grins. "Very well. What nickname do you have for me, Miss?"

I roll my eyes at the name. "Okay, first, no more of this 'Miss' shit. You can call me Seph."

Beta lifts a brow. "Seph? That sounds a little personal. You wouldn't rather us call you Persephone?"

I want to shake my head but can't since he's still drawing on my face. My chest clenches with fear at my next words. "No. I want you to call me Seph. I . . . I don't have many friends. And . . . since we will be spending a lot of time together, I figured . . ." I huff out a breath, which ruffles Beta's long hair. I feel like he's a man bun kind of guy.

His eyes meet mine before he smiles again. "You want to be friends with us?"

I try not to move my head as I shrug. "What better friends to have than the top dogs in Hades' Hellhound Crew. Plus . . . I feel like you guys would be awesome friends to have."

Beta snickers as he pulls away, taking in his work. His eyes meet mine, and his face grows serious. "It's dangerous to be friends with us."

I hum. "Well, I'm sure it's dangerous to be friends with me too."

He taps the end of the brush to his lips as he nods. "I suppose you have a point. Okay, I think you're ready."

He helps me down from the counter, and I take a deep breath before turning to look at myself in the mirror. My jaw drops when I see my reflection. One side of my face is the outline of a skull, and the other has intricate flowers. It's perfect. My eyes meet Beta's, and I whisper, "Thank you, Jax."

His eyes widen at his name, then he gives me a soft smile. "You're welcome, Jane," he whispers back.

My eyes meet Alpha's in the mirror, and I watch as he closes the bathroom door. He turns to meet my gaze in the mirror before saying, "It's safe to talk."

I don't whisper my next words. "How am I supposed to be Persephone, Silas? I've spent the last ten years just trying to survive. I've been hiding for so long that I don't know if I can do this."

I watch Silas' stern face soften as he replies, "You're not Jane right now. You're Persephone. You can do this."

"What if I fuck it up?!"

Jax grips my shoulders and replies, "The woman I saw downstairs wasn't Jane. She was Persephone. She was strong and took charge."

I take a deep breath, trying to embody that woman again. Silas opens the door and nods to me. "Don't try so hard to be her; you already are her."

Jax gives my shoulders one last squeeze before backing away. "You've got this, Seph."

I can't help but grin at the nickname. Clapping my hands together, I nod. Grabbing my heels from the counter, I slip them on. I look back up to find that Jax and Silas have put their contacts in. I snort out a laugh. "You guys do know you look creepy as fuck with those contacts in, right?"

Silas gives me a devilish grin and leaves the bathroom. "That's the point," he calls over his shoulder.

I shrug. I suppose that is the point. Jax gives me a nod before following after his brother. I follow behind them, and with each step I take, I feel a little bit better. With the click of my heels against the floor, Persephone comes alive.

Resuming our roles, Alpha allows me to walk in front, but not far enough ahead that he couldn't pull me to safety at a moment's notice.

I hear Beta's whispered words behind me, "Get it, Seph." I snort a laugh when I hear a grunt.

"Shut the fuck up," Alpha whisper shouts.

"What?" Beta whispers, "I was just giving her a little confidence boost before she walks into a room full of demons."

Entering the room, I pause for a moment. Jace looks every bit the part of Hades as he stands by his throne. Howe stands guard on the other side like Cerberus is meant to do. Alec is by the door to deliver people like Charon is meant to do. And lastly, there's Zane. He looks like the god of death, Thanatos.

The room suddenly goes dark before UV lights shine. All of their facial tattoos shine in the darkness. I look back to find Jace holding out a hand for me. He has a soft smile as he says, "Hello, My Queen."

I make my way over and slide my hand into his. He gives it a soft kiss before he nods to his throne. "Have a seat, Persephone."

Interesting, but I do as I'm told. Once I'm seated, Jace sits on the arm of the chair, and Howe stands a little closer to my other side.

"Our first person of the night wishes for an audience. Would you like me to deliver them to you, My Queen?" Alec asks.

I look over to Jace, confused by the question. Am I in charge tonight? He lifts a brow. "Charon asked a question, Persephone. You are in charge tonight."

Suddenly empowered by this change, I sit up straighter. I cross my legs and lean to the side closest to Howe. I smile at Alec as I say, "Bring us the souls who wish to barter with death, Charon."

Chapter Seventeen

JANE

Two hours later, we were done with our audiences. I take a deep breath before saying, "We need to talk. Is there somewhere we can go that's secure?"

The guys all exchange glances before Jace nods. "We can go to the war room. It's usually where we talk strategy."

I nod as the lights flick back on. Blinking a few times, I let my eyes adjust to the bright light. I see that Alpha and Beta are in the corner of the room, so I point to them and say, "You two are coming to the meeting too."

They both nod, and Alpha opens the door for us to leave. The two lead us to the war room and close the door once everyone is inside. "Do we still need to use code names in here?"

Beta holds up a hand and presses on his earpiece. "Secure war room." There's a pause before a quiet and steady hum fills the room. He nods to us. "Room is secure."

I've been holding onto my anger over the whole bulletproof vest thing for the last few hours. But my anger isn't as fiery as before. I sigh as I begin, "First off, I'm still angry about the whole bulletproof vest thing."

Jace tries to say something, but I don't let him interrupt. "I know why you did it. Still doesn't excuse the fact that you guys didn't tell me about the danger happening right now."

I point to Silas and Jax. "You two are now my bodyguards, and with that, I expect you to be honest and upfront with me. My men will try to hide things from me . . ."

Howe groans but says, "We won't hide things from you anymore."

I roll my eyes but continue. "They will unintentionally hide things from me, not realizing they could be important. I expect you two to tell me what I need to know, even if it's something you don't want me to know."

They both nod as Silas says, "Understood, Miss."

I arch a brow at him. "What did I say about the 'Miss' thing?"

I see the twitch of his lip. "Understood, Persephone."

I snort out a laugh. Stubborn man. I suppose that's as good as it's going to get. Turning back to my men, I demand, "Now. What's going on?"

They all look at each other before Jace sighs and answers, "We are having issues with a gang from another territory. They seem to have been bought out and support our current government."

"They won't support them any longer when they find themselves dead," Howe grumbles.

Zane snorts. "Hard to support a government after they get what they want and kill you in payment."

I arch a brow and ask the obvious question. "Don't they realize they will be killed once the officials get what they want?"

Jax speaks up behind me, "Money talks, Sweets. I'm sure the officials made promises, and this gang is stupid enough to believe them."

I hum in agreement. Money does talk, unfortunately. Loyalty is hard to find. "Anything else I should know about?"

"We have a Hound undercover in the government right now. Seems your dad has been making some inquiries about you in the Underground." Zane says, then shoots a pointed look behind me, so I turn to look at Silas and Jax.

Silas nods. "We have been controlling the situation. We have several men keeping an eye on him. We will know what he's doing and what he's asking."

Jax must see the fear in my eyes because he says, "We won't let him get his hands on you. He'll have to get through several Hounds. Excluding us. At least one of us will be with you at all times."

Alec adds, "Plus, you have us, Moonbeam."

"Moonbeam?" Jax teases with a smirk.

I feel my cheeks heat as I grumble, "It's a childhood nickname."

His smirk grows into a grin. "Ah, and what are your other nicknames?"

I hear Howe laugh and answer, "Starlight."

Zane grunts out, "Sunshine."

I wait for Jace to say his, but he doesn't. I look up to meet his eyes, and he smirks as he says, "Princess."

Jax roars with laughter. "Princess?!"

I turn to glare at Jax and put my hands on my hips. "And that nickname will NEVER cross your lips. I hate that nickname."

"Which is why he does it, I'm sure." Jax smirks.

"Asshole," I grunt.

Jax grins and says, "We all got 'em."

I can't help but smile as I say, "Little shit."

He grins even wider. "We all do it."

Yep, he and I were going to get along just fine. Best of friends. I look at Silas and ask, "What were your plans tonight? Don't you guys ever go home?"

He seems surprised by my question but answers, "The original plan was to go home this evening and help Luka with a few things. But with what's going on now . . ."

I wave off his concern. "Go home. Help Luka with what needs to be done for the Underground."

He looks over my shoulder, and I know he's looking at Jace for confirmation. I wait to see if Jace will contradict my orders, but instead, he says, "Do what she says. We will make sure one of us is with her at all times. Update me if there is anything I should take care of."

Silas nods and turns to leave. Jax gives me a salute and follows behind. Before they leave, I say, "I expect to meet Luka soon." I've never actually met their youngest brother. I'd only seen him on TV briefly when I'd managed to stay somewhere with a TV or in passing at places I worked. But I hadn't seen him much in the last year or so. I know his eyes match his brothers, and he had short, spiky hair the last time I saw him. He usually wore jeans and a leather jacket to events.

Silas and Jax changed their looks too. While here, they wear their contacts to cover their natural hazel eyes. Silas wears all black from head to toe. On TV, I noticed that his dark brown hair was usually slicked back so that you could see the shaved sides of his head. But here, he wears it in Viking braids so it won't get in the way. His tattoos are completely covered too. Jax's hair goes past his shoulders when down and combed over to one side, showing off his shaved side. I noticed on TV that he wore it in a bun with several strands wisping out. I'm sure that plays into his playboy image. He also wears gloves when here to cover up his hand tattoos.

Jax waves a hand over his head and calls, "Will do. We can meet up at the house."

"Sounds great," I yell as they leave. My focus switches back to my guys, and I walk over to one of the chairs and sit my ass down. Fuck, I love these heels, but they are a killer on my feet. I slip out of them and toss them on the table.

Howe comes over and sits in front of me before grabbing one of my feet. He starts massaging it, and I can't stop the moan that slips out. I hear him snicker, but I don't care. "This doesn't mean I forgive you yet," I mumble.

"Yes, it does," he disagrees, then laughs.

I groan again as he hits another sore spot. Fuck, he's right; I do. I forgave them all already. Doesn't mean I can't make them work for it. "Fine, but only because you're giving me a great massage."

Fingers start massaging my shoulders, and I'm instantly putty in their hands. I hear Alec's chuckle behind me as he teases, "What about me?"

"Mmhmm," is all I manage. I'm not sure if it sounded like a yes, but I am enjoying this massage too much.

"Are we good, Sunshine?" Zane asks from beside me.

My eyes open enough to see him hovering beside me. I mumble, "Say you love me again."

I see the tilt of his lip as he bends down and kisses my forehead. My eyes close as his lips land next to my ear, and he says, "I love you, Sunshine."

I smile as I say, "I love you too." I feel him pull away, and suddenly, all of the hands on my body stop. I'm about to whine when I'm lifted in the air. My eyes shoot open to see Jace holding me and making his way out of the war room.

Settling into his arms, I lay my head against his chest. "What about me?" he whispers.

I snuggle in closer as I say, "As long as you keep me in the loop in the future. We are a team now."

I feel his lips against my head as he says, "I promise, My Queen."

Chapter Eighteen

JANE

It's been a week since I found my guys again, and I still can't believe it. I'm currently running around the house trying to get everything ready. The guys invited the Steepe brothers over for a BBQ, and I want to make sure everything is perfect, but the guys think it's funny that I am trying so hard.

"Stop worrying so much," Jace says from the couch.

"I just want everything to go okay," I whine.

Howe rubs my shoulders and asks, "Why are you stressing so much? We see them at work all the time."

I huff a sigh. "I don't know. I guess . . . I just want everything to go okay. These are the first friends I've had in like ten years. I want to make a good impression."

Zane grunts. "Silas and Jax like you already."

I groan. "How do you know?"

He shrugs. "Just do. I can tell they respect you. Jax seems to have taken a liking to you, and Silas doesn't interact with many people, but he seems to talk to you. Luka is easygoing; you'll have no problem with him."

"He probably won't look anything like them, though. He'll be wearing something different than he normally wears for the public. He doesn't want anyone to know he's affiliated with Silas and Jax when they are posing as Alpha and Beta," Alec adds.

Howe hums his agreement. "True. He'll probably change once he gets inside, though. I know he hates the shit he has to wear when he's under-cover."

The bell rings, and I jump. Damnit! Why the fuck am I so jumpy? Howe gives my shoulders a squeeze before giving me a kiss on the cheek. "It will be okay." He releases my shoulders and makes his way over to the door.

I wipe my hands on my sweater dress, trying to make sure I don't have any wrinkles. I look up when I hear Silas' voice. "Hey, thanks for inviting us over."

Zane and Jace give him a handshake, then Howe and Alec give him one of those tough bro hugs. Silas sees me over by the kitchen and gives me a nod and a small smile.

I take a deep breath before smiling back. "Hey, Silas." I make my way over to him. He reaches up, puts a hand on my head, then messes up my hair. I swat at his hand with a scratch as I mutter, "Don't fuck up my hair, dickhead."

He grunts out a laugh. "Much better."

I roll my eyes but smile as he walks around me and leans against the kitchen island. I turn just in time to let out a squeak when Jax picks me up in a hug. I squeal in laughter as he spins. He laughs as he sets me down. "Hey, Sweets!"

"Hey, Jax."

He shifts and holds out a hand to the door, saying, "As promised, we have brought Luka."

My jaw drops when I see the man who walks through the door. He doesn't look like the Luka I've seen on TV. Instead, he looks like . . . a man from my past. "Ben?" I ask in a whispered voice.

His blue eyes meet mine, and his brows furrow as he says, "I haven't used that name in years. To be honest, I haven't used that name since . . ." He squints at me for a moment, and then his eyes widen. He quickly walks over to me before reaching out a hand but pauses before he touches my face. "Emma?"

I can't stop the smile that spreads across my face as I jump on him. I wrap my arms around his neck and say, "It's been so fucking long!" I pull away, looking at his face.

His grin is enormous as he gives me one last squeeze before putting me down. He shakes his head, letting out a laugh. "Girl! You've changed your hair. It used to be red, right? And you had green eyes." He steps away and makes a twirling motion with his finger. "Give me a twirl."

I laugh as I spin around, then stop in front of him. He snorts a laugh as he teases, "I like the new hair. You weren't much of a redhead."

I slap his chest. "I made more money as a redhead, and you know it!"

He rolls his eyes before he says, "You would have made money with any hair color, Em. Although, I guess your name isn't Emma, is it?"

I grin, holding out my hand. "I'm Jane. I'm officially the Queen of the Underworld."

He matches my grin as he shakes my hand. "Luka Steepe. I run the Underground with my brothers."

A growl behind me makes me realize I've completely forgotten we have an audience. I turn to find everyone staring at Luka and me.

Silas is the first one to break the silence. "How do you know each other?"

Jace growls. "Yeah, how do you know our girl?"

I look at Luka before sighing. Guess I will need to tell my boys about my past sooner than I thought. I rub the back of my neck as I awkwardly explain. "Well, when I was on the run from my dad, I needed to make some money somehow." I point to Luka beside me. "I met him at a strip club. He must have seen how desperate I was because he gave me a job."

"He's seen you fucking naked?!" Zane yells.

"Fuck no," Luka says with a grunt beside me. "She wasn't allowed to strip naked. Our women only strip naked if they choose to. But I knew the guys at the club would eat her alive if she did. So instead, she was one of the girls who danced in the cages above the main stage. Men couldn't touch her."

Seeing that this conversion is headed nowhere good, I hold up a hand, trying to get my guys to stop. I sigh and say, "Can we shelve this conversion until later? I want to have fun, and this is turning into a depressing recollection of my past."

The guys look between themselves before turning back to me with a nod. I huff out another sigh. "Great. Can we get some food going now? I'm getting hungry."

***

In the end, we had a great time. Everyone talked for hours, and it felt like a bunch of friends having a night together. I loved every moment of it. Silas, Jax, and Luka waved goodbye as they got into their vehicle and left.

Now I'm snuggled up on the couch. I know I can't avoid the questions any longer, as much as I wish the guys would have forgotten.

Jace is the first to ask, "What happened over the last few years?"

I give him a half-hearted shrug. "I ran away from Dad. I had to find a way to keep myself alive, so I took random jobs. Unfortunately, not all of them were jobs I'm proud of, but I got paid."

"That isn't much to go on," Alec says as he snuggles up beside me on the couch.

"I don't really want to reminisce on past jobs I had. I survived and managed to keep my dad's eyes off of me," I pause for a moment before asking, "What I'm curious about is what happened with you guys the past ten years."

"Not much to tell, Princess."

I snort out a laugh. Jace's dismissal will not work for me. "I'm not buying it. I know you guys aren't fucking saints. Just tell me what happened after I left."

Surprisingly, it's Alec who speaks up first. "I killed my dad a year later."

My eyes widen. Holy shit. I mean, I'm not exactly surprised. I wouldn't call the man his dad; he was their foster dad. But that fucker was disgusting. He had done things to the guys; I know he did. Worst of all to Alec. Alec had been the smallest of the guys, and their foster dad took advantage of that.

Alec continues as if he didn't just drop that bomb on me. "We all dropped out of school when we were, like, sixteen, I think. We made Howe get his GED, though. He was always the smartest out of us."

I look over at the man in question. He shrugs. "I was able to hack into the local community colleges and take several classes for free. I have degrees in cybersecurity along with chemistry and firearms technology."

Well, fuck . . . that explains a lot of things. I look between Jace and Zane since they still haven't said anything. "Jace. Tell me what happened." I didn't mean for the words to come out whiny, but they did.

He sighs, then growls and says, "Fine, you want to know our dark and dirty past, Princess? I'll tell you."

Chapter Nineteen

JACE

Four years ago...

It has taken fucking years to get to this point. Years. We've fought every local gang in the area starting five years ago. Every one of them is now under my control. Under Hades' control. But having all this power was doing shit to help with what I wanted it for. We want to find Jane, but her dad did a great job of fucking hiding her. I slam my fingers on the keys of my piano, but I can't fucking play. Well, I could. Just not the song I wanted to play. My phone rings, interrupting my thoughts.

Without looking at who it is, I pick up and bark, "What?"

Howe's voice comes over the line. "Get the fuck up to security. I found her."

I jump up from the piano bench. I must not have heard him correctly. "What?"

"I fucking found her!" he says again.

I race out of my room and up the stairs. I don't hang up the phone. Instead, I ask, "How the fuck did you find her? Her dad has basically erased her from existence."

I hear a growl in his voice as he spits out, "Seems Mr. Alexander has finally decided to make use of his daughter."

Rushing into the security room, I look around at all the screens Howe has up. I slam my phone down, anger rushing through me when I see where he found Jane. "The Underground bidding site?"

Howe clicks a few buttons and pulls up her ad. "Much worse," he admits.

"Seventeen-year-old heiress for sale. No longer a virgin, but still ripe." I can't believe what the fuck I'm reading. "Is he trying to sell her off like fucking cattle?"

Howe scrolls further down. "It seems he's trying to sell her off to breed her."

"Because that's better!" I scream. Howe flinches, and I instantly deflate. Fuck. "I'm sorry, Cerberus."

He nods in understanding. "I know, Hades. How do you want to proceed?"

I straighten. "Call Luka, and see if he can get the posting taken down. I know he can control the postings from his side of things better than you can from this side. We will send some Hounds out to get her."

It was too late. Too fucking late. She was gone. Somehow she figured out what her dad was planning and left. Howe has spent hours looking through footage from every street cam in the territory in an attempt to find her, but nothing. She vanished. She's a ghost. I feel like fucking shit because I already told Alec and Zane about her. That we finally found her. And now . . . she's gone. Slipped through our fucking fingers once more.

I look out over the city as I sit on the cliff behind the Cave. It's the only spot I can think. I wish I had Alec's and Howe's optimism. They immediately said that it was not a problem. We would be able to find her again. But will we? I feel someone slide up next to me, and without looking, I know who it is.

"You doing okay, brother?"

Zane's gruff voice doesn't hide his disappointment. He and I are the same. We embraced the darkness when she was taken from us. We continue to live in the dark. I sigh and say, "About as well as you are, I'm sure."

He hums. "She's Sunshine. She can't hide forever. She's too bright."

I can tell he is forcing himself to try to be positive. But I know better. "I'm starting to think it's too dark to find the sunshine anymore, brother. She's turned into a ghost."

Zane is quiet for a moment before he says, "The light can't shine as brightly without the dark."

I snort out a humorless laugh. "Have Cerberus and Charon rubbed off on you, brother?"

He huffs out a deep sigh and replies, "Truthfully? I'm trying not to be consumed by the darkness myself."

My gaze shifts to him, and I notice the dullness in his eyes. He's becoming Thanatos, the god of death. I bump his shoulder, trying to stop the darkness from taking hold of him. His eyes shift to mine before he whispers, "I can't settle for a ghost anymore. I need my Sunshine."

Chapter Twenty

JANE

I'm a bit speechless. They had found me, and I didn't even know. I had slipped through their fingers. I could have been with them four years ago. But would I be the same Jane I am now if I hadn't gone through what I had over the last four years? I don't think I would. Huffing out a sigh, I grab a pillow and cuddle it in my lap.

They opened up about some of their past; the least I could do was tell them more about what I'd been through. I suppose since we were on the subject of Luka and me, maybe that would be a good place to start.

I feel Howe slide onto the couch on my other side. Now snuggled between Howe and Alec, I feel myself relaxing without meaning to. I am curious about their relationship, but that's a question for another time.

Taking a deep breath, I try to exhale my reservations about sharing my past. It was the past. It's not like I can change it. Looking between my guys, I say, "I'm not going to tell you everything that happened over the last ten years we've been separated. Most of it I would like to forget. Especially the time I spent with my dad." I can't stop the shiver of disgust that runs down my spine. I knew I would have to tell them some stuff, but it didn't need to be today.

Alec slides his hand into mine and says softly, "You don't have to share anything if you don't want to."

I give his hand a squeeze and flash him a small smile before responding. "I don't mind. Some things are just more painful to bring up. But I can share what happened between Luka and me. It's not a horrible memory. It's actually one of the better memories I have."

Howe cuddles closer, wrapping an arm around the back of my head. I feel Alec stiffen and then relax beside me. I look over to see that Howe has tangled his fingers in Alec's short hair. Fuck, I really want to hear their story. Another time. "Tell us, Starlight."

"Alright." I sigh. "So here's how I met Luka . . ."

Three and a half years ago...

Shit, I need to get a job. These odd jobs aren't cutting it anymore, and I need money if I am going to travel the territory in search of my guys. But no one wants to hire a seventeen-year-old. Even though I am almost eighteen and look like I am older. I could pass for a twenty-year-old if I really needed to.

I only have ten bucks in my pocket, but that isn't going to get me anywhere to stay for the night. Huffing out a sigh, I look around the busy streets. Maybe I could . . . there! The neon lights read, Tartarus. I know it is a strip club, but it is a high-end strip club. It is part of the underground owned by the Underworld. I know they treat their ladies well and pay even better.

Fuck it. May as well give it a shot. Pulling up my big girl panties, I walk towards the club. Metaphorically speaking, anyways. I didn't actually pull up my big girl panties because I am not currently wearing any. I am not a man. I do not flip them inside out and wear them again. Nor do I wear them until they stink. Fucking gross.

Taking a deep breath, I open the doors to the club, and I'm instantly bombarded with thumping music. This is one of those moments I hope I don't look like I feel. Because I feel like shit.

Making my way over to the bar, I take a seat. What the fuck is my plan? Just march in here and demand to talk to the owner? Fucking hell, Jane, great plan. I take a minute to look around. The club is dark and lit with red LED lights and chains dangling from the ceiling. The furniture is chrome and black leather. A few cages hang from the ceiling with girls dancing to the pulsing beat. Some are clothed, while others are completely naked.

A husky voice behind me startles me out of my thoughts, and I turn to look at the bartender. Holy Shit. Fucking hell, this man is sexy. I suppose the tight leather pants and leather shirt he is wearing . . . can you call it a shirt? It barely covers his nipples while the sleeves cut off at his forearms. But damn, it shows off his assets.

He clears his throat, and I look up to see him smirking at me. Well . . . shit. "Sorry," I squeak out.

He grins and asks, "What can I do for you?"

Trying to keep my eyes above his nips, I say, "I need to talk to the owner."

He raises a brow. "The owner? Why's that, Sugar?"

I bite my lip and tell him, "I need a job."

He looks me up and down before saying, "You don't look old enough to be in this establishment, let alone work here."

I groan. "I know. But I really need the money."

"Don't we all, Sugar Tits? But the owner is too busy to tell you exactly what I'm telling you now. You're too young."

"Please. I understand that you can't have me on your books legally, but—"

He arches a brow. "You want us to pay you under the table?"

I nod. "I need the money. This place wouldn't even be on his radar to . . ." Fuck! I snap my lips shut. Fuck! Great going Jane.

He leans on the bar and asks, "Are you in trouble, Sugar?" I don't answer. Fuck, Jane! He leans closer before saying, "You need to tell me if you're in trouble. I can't help otherwise."

I huff out a sigh before nodding. He looks at me for a moment as if he's trying to figure me out before nodding. "Stay here. I'll be back."

I sit and wait, anxiously twiddling my fingers. Once I ran, I changed my hair color and even my eye color in an attempt to make sure my dad doesn't find me. With red hair and green eyes, I no longer look anything like my old self.

Hearing two people talking, I look up. As I watch, the barman walks back in my direction with another man behind him. The other guy is wearing leather pants. He's also wearing a leather vest with nothing underneath. His brown hair is slicked back, and when his eyes meet mine, they remind me of my own. Well, my old eyes but brighter. Bright blue.

He gives me a nod before introducing himself, "I'm Ben, the owner of this club. Creed says you need some help. Says you're running from someone."

I can't stop the glare I shoot the bartender. He just smiles as he shrugs. Mumbling a few choice words, I grind my teeth before admitting, "Yes, I'm running."

"Who you running from?"

I cross my arms over my chest as I say, "Who I'm running from is none of your concern."

He arches a brow and replies, "It is my business if I allow you to work for me. Now I'm only asking once more, who you running from, girl?"

I debate my options for a moment before caving. "I'm running from my dad. I refuse to let him sell me like I'm a fucking heifer to breed. I'm not property."

He looks at me, considering me for a moment before saying, "Red hair is recognizable."

I point to my hair. "This isn't my natural color. Not even close. And before you ask, my eye color is different too."

He taps his chin thoughtfully before asking, "Do you dance?"

I shrug noncommittally. "I haven't got any complaints yet."

He smirks. "Okay, here's the deal; I'll provide you food and board. You get to keep your tips." He points up at the ceiling and continues. "You *will* be in a cage during your shift. No exceptions. Bra and underwear stay on. Tits and vag are for twenty-one and older, which you are not."

He looks over to Creed, and the man gives him a nod. "I'll keep an eye on her, boss."

He turns back to me, holding out a hand. "Do we have a deal?"

I look at his hand, hesitating for only a moment before sliding my hand into his. "Deal."

"What's your name, kid?"

Fuck, what name am I going by now? It's . . . "Emma."

He quirks a brow, knowing that it has to be a fake name, before shrugging. "Emma. Hum. The Ember from Tartarus herself. I'm sure you'll get lots of customers with that tagline. Emma the Ember from Tartarus."

Chapter Twenty-One

JANE

Present Day

I let out a long yawn before looking around at the guys. My brows knit together when I see their frowning faces. They look irritated. "Why do you look like someone pissed in your chocolatey pebbles?"

Jace arches a brow. "Pissed in our chocolatey pebbles?"

I nod. "You look irritated."

"We are irritated," Zane confirms in a huff.

"Why the hell are you irritated? You are the ones who wanted to know what happened."

Alec sighs heavily and explains, "You just told us that you worked at one of our clubs. If we had kept up on our club visits, we would have known you were there."

I shake my head. "I completely changed my look. You wouldn't have recognized me even if you had visited."

"Still doesn't help with the fact that you were so close, and we didn't even know," Howe says with a growl.

"Why did you leave Tartarus?" Jace asks.

"Ben, well, I guess he wasn't really Ben. Luka was charged to take over a different club after a year and a half. He didn't trust the new guy in charge to keep me off the floor, so when he left, he recommended another club I could work at that would provide me with a little protection." I snuggle closer into the couch. "I only stayed there for a few months before moving to a different location."

"So . . . what other jobs did you work?" Howe asks.

I shrug. "I usually worked at bars and strip clubs. It was easier to blend in. People didn't ask a lot of questions. I usually picked places I knew my father wouldn't visit but didn't stay in one place too long in case he had people looking for me." I stifle another yawn before resting my head on the back of the couch.

Suddenly, I'm lifted into the air. I didn't realize I had closed my eyes until I opened them to see what was happening. Jace is carrying me towards his bedroom, so I smile, closing my eyes and snuggling into his chest.

His chest rumbles as he asks softly, "Do you mind being mine for the night, Princess?"

Shaking my head, I say, "Not at all." I'm still half asleep as I feel myself being lowered and sigh when I'm laid on a very comfortable bed. I snuggle into the bed and one of the pillows that smell heavily of his woodsy scent.

He snuggles up behind me, spooning me, and throws the blanket over us. I can feel his warm breath on my neck as he takes deep breaths. Letting it out with a deep sigh, he snuggles closer.

As my body relaxes, I feel myself sink into the bed. I have never felt as safe as I do with my boys. Although, I suppose they aren't boys anymore. I don't even realize I've fallen asleep till I wake up the next morning.

Jace stirs behind me and presses a soft kiss on my neck. His voice is rough from sleep as he says, "Morning, Princess."

"Morning," I say with a smirk. I can't stop myself from rubbing my ass against his conveniently placed morning wood. I snicker when he groans.

"Don't play games, Princess," he warns as he presses his cock roughly against my ass.

"What if I want to play games?" I whisper. He shifts away from me just far enough to push up on his elbow and look down at me.

He arches a brow. "You want to play?"

There's a tilt to my lips as I respond, "You were horrible to play with as a kid. You had no clue how to have fun. Has that changed, Jace?"

His eyes darken with lust as he teases, "So you want to have fun, do you?"

My tongue darts out to moisten my lips, and I watch his eyes follow the movement. "If you don't want to have fun with me, I can always go find Alec and Howe. They will always play with me."

I squeal when I'm suddenly flipped onto my back, and Jace hovers above me. He slams his lips to mine, and I groan in pleasure. He hungrily kisses me as he grinds his cock against my clit. I gasp when he pulls away. He looks down at me with a satisfied smirk and says, "You shouldn't tease the ruler of the Underworld, Princess."

I slide my fingers into his jet-black hair and tug roughly. He lets out a groan as I smirk up at him. "You shouldn't tease the Queen of the Underworld, Little Prince."

He growls as he sits up and rips off my underwear. When had I gotten undressed? I could have sworn I was dressed when I went to bed. I must have been too sleepy to realize he had stripped me out of my clothes.

He slides the cups of my bra up and massages my breasts. My back bows into his touch, and I moan. I impatiently slide my hands down his body, trying to get his underwear off, but he jumps off the bed and rips them off before I can.

Holy. Fuck. His dick is pierced. His extremely-hard dick stands tall, proudly showing off his four piercings. I think the piercing is called a Jacob's Ladder. "Your dick is pierced," I comment helpfully.

He smirks as he jumps back onto the bed. "It is."

"Didn't that fucking hurt?" I ask curiously.

He arches a surprised brow. "Are we seriously discussing this right now?"

"It's a serious question!" He rolls his eyes and grinds against my clit again. My mind blanks, and I moan loudly. "Nevermind. Not important."

"That's what I thought." He snickers, then bends down and captures one of my nipples with his mouth.

Tangling my fingers in his hair, I lie there panting. His fingers slowly glide down my belly until his hand is between his dick and my clit, then he rubs the nub slowly. I groan, and my fingers tighten in his hair.

He switches to my other nipple as he shifts his hand to push a finger into my cunt. Fuck! Fuck! That feels amazing! He pumps slowly as he inserts another finger. He cups his hand in just the right way so that the top of his palm is rubbing against my clit.

"Faster," I pant. I can feel my body tightening already.

He doesn't do what I want, though. Instead, he inserts another finger, slowly pumping into me while rubbing my clit. Then he bites down hard on my nipple, and I instantly combust.

I didn't realize I had closed my eyes, but when I open them, I find Jace pulling away and sliding his fingers out of my dripping cunt. He stares into my eyes for a moment, then sticks his tongue out to show off the skull ball on his tongue. He gives me a naughty smirk and wraps his tongue around his fingers that were inside of me, sucking away the evidence of my orgasms.

Fucking hell. Who knew that was fucking sexy. I continue to watch, panting with my growing need.

He grins down at me and teasingly asks, "Do you want something more, Princess?"

Growling, I can't stop myself from demanding, "Fuck me like you missed me, Hades!" I'm not sure why I chose to use his code name, but with the heat that flares in his eyes, I'm not sure I care.

He moves so he's hovering over me and places his cock at my entrance. "As you wish, Persephone." Without warning, he slams into me all the way to the hilt. My fingers dig into his back, and he lets out a deep groan. He smashes his lips to mine in hunger as he pulls out and slams into me again.

Each time he thrusts back inside me, I moan, and he swallows them down as he devours my mouth. My fingers find his hair, and I tug. He growls into my mouth, then pulls away. He's panting as he looks down at me. I can see sweat beading on his forehead, and his hair is damp. I didn't realize how hot it was in this room till now.

He punctuates each word he says next as he pounds into me. "I. Fucking. Missed. You."

I moan as I feel myself tighten around him. I'm panting as I say, "I missed you too."

He growls, and his movements grow more frantic. Slamming his lips to mine again, his fingers find my clit. He rubs the sensitive bud, and I can't stop the orgasm from taking over my body as I clamp around him.

Capturing my scream of ecstasy with his mouth, he continues milking my orgasm. I roughly tug on his hair, and he pulls back before slamming into me with a roar of ecstasy. He pumps a few more times before closing his eyes and pressing his forehead against mine.

Our panting breaths mingle at this moment. He pulls away, opening his eyes to look into mine. I notice his eyes don't look as dark as they normally do. They look more like milk chocolate rather than the dark chocolate they usually are. He gazes down at me as if trying to memorize how I look at this moment.

I feel a bit shy under his gaze, so I ask, "Why are you staring at me?"

His lips tilt as he simply says, "Memorizing." With a groan, he slips out of me and slides off the bed.

"Memorizing what?" I ask, sitting up in bed as I watch him turn around to look at me again.

"You." He holds a hand out to me. "Would you like to take a shower with me?"

I slide out of bed, placing my hand in his. "Me? And yeah, I could go for a shower."

He nods as he pulls me into his bathroom. But he didn't answer my question, so I ask again, "Why were you memorizing me?"

He looks over his shoulder at me, and the look in his eyes makes me stumble. His voice is barely more than a whisper when he says, "If I have to settle for a memory again . . . I want to make sure I memorize everything I can about you."

Chapter Twenty-Two

JANE

I really need to get out of the shower, but what Jace said has me pausing. Did he say that because he thinks I will leave or that something will eventually happen to me? I understand that this line of work is dangerous. That's why Howe has been giving me lessons on different martial arts moves.

Letting out a sigh, I shut off the water. It's time to get out and get ready for the day. I should be excited for today; it is the day I finally get my Persephone tattoos. Well, a few of them. The guys don't want me to get my face tattooed yet. I told them I could handle the pain, but they said it would take a while to heal, so I settled for getting other tattoos instead.

I also explained to them that I had gotten several tattoos and piercings over the years to help with my cover. I could handle pain. But to avoid an argument, I wasn't getting my facial tattoo today. Although, Jace had told me that their tattoo artist uses a new numbing gel. The artist can do larger tattoos and longer sessions since the client can't feel anything. Considering I am getting one on my back and both my hands, I figure that will work in my favor.

Looking in the mirror, I debate what jewelry to wear today. The guys had bought so much. My nasallang piercing has two simple diamond studs with a silver chain across my nose. Jace had ordered me jewelry with a skull for my belly button piercing, which I haven't changed since I got it pierced.

It is fucking cute. I settle on a dark pink flower for my eyebrow piercing since it feels like a Persephone thing to wear. Lastly, I settle on a pair of dangling teardrop earrings. I know shit could hit the fan today, but that doesn't mean I can't look cute.

I slip into a low-back dress and slide my feet into a pair of sandals considering everything going on right now. I know we are still having issues with the gang from another territory. Huffing out a sigh, I also put on the bulletproof vest. I'm not sure if I will be able to put it back on once I get the tattoos, though. Guess one of the guys will have to protect me should the need arise. We are planning on returning to the house, though, so it shouldn't be a problem. Hopefully.

Leaving my room, I walk down the hallway and the stairs. I am greeted by the guys waiting in the living room. Jace is in a white button-down with a vest and black slacks. Zane is wearing a pair of gray sweatpants and a black hoodie. Well fuck. Do guys not realize what wearing sweatpants does to a girl? Catching myself before I start drooling, I turn my attention to Alec. He's in a pair of dark-wash jeans and a loose-fitting white t-shirt. I look at Howe last. If I thought sweatpants were sexy . . . holy shit. Howe fills out the pair of black joggers he's wearing perfectly. He has on a tight tank and a hoodie wrapped around his waist.

I point to the hoodie and ask, "Why do you have a hoodie tied around your waist instead of wearing it?"

He smirks at me. "I get hot if I wear a hoodie. It's chilly outside, so I'll need it, but I'll take it off once we get to the tattoo shop."

I shrug; I suppose that makes sense. I tap my bulletproof vest and say, "I'm not sure I'll be able to put this back on after I get my back tattoo."

Zane hands me my jacket. "We shouldn't have any issues. The shop is deep within our territory. The other gang would be stupid if they tried to infiltrate that area. We have too many paid personnel around there."

I slip into my jacket and follow the guys out the front door. Alpha and Beta are there waiting for us, and I can't stop smirking as I tease, "So you're on babysitting duty today?"

Jax rolls his eyes as he opens the back door of the large SUV for me. "I wouldn't call it babysitting if it's our job to protect the main Underworld crew."

I wait until he slips into the passenger seat, and Silas slides into the driver's seat before asking, "So what would you consider babysitting?"

Smirking at me over his shoulder, he replies, "When we have to look after you."

I roll my eyes as Silas snorts from the driver's seat. I switch my gaze to him. "Do you have anything to add, Si?"

"Si?" He briefly looks at me in the rearview mirror before focusing on the road again.

I shrug. "Yeah. It's my nickname for you now. I told you I would come up with one, didn't I?"

He grunts and grumbles, "I didn't think you were serious."

Jax laughs. "That was your first mistake, brother." He shifts to look at me better and asks, "Did you come up with a nickname for me?"

I shake my head. "Not yet. I can't call you J because that's what I call Jace."

He shrugs and turns around in his chair to face the road again. "I'm sure you'll come up with something."

I notice they are both in their uniforms, so I'm assuming I can't call them by their real names in public.

About twenty minutes later, we arrive at the tattoo shop. Alpha and Beta get out first to ensure the area is clear before Beta opens the door for us and says, "All clear, boss."

Jace nods and exits the car first. Zane follows next. They stand on either side of the door, waiting as I get out, followed closely by Alec and Howe.

I'm surprised by the tattoo shop as we enter. The front is lit with different colored LED lights with varying spray-painted art covering the walls.

I'm about to ask how anyone could possibly work here, considering how dark it is, until I'm escorted into a private room that's well lit. The walls are covered with pictures of what I assume this artist is known for.

I sit down on the chair in the middle of the room as my guys move to stand against the far wall. Looking over my shoulder, I find Alpha and Beta guarding the door from the outside. My eyes widen when the artist walks in. With the way the guys talked about them, I was expecting a man, but I was wrong.

The only way I can describe the woman who walks in is stunning. Her light chocolate skin is covered in intricate artwork. Some of it is done using color, and others are black and grayscale art pieces. Her hair is light blue and done up in three tight buns that run down the center of her head. She looks at me with a smile. "You were expecting a guy, weren't you?"

I flush as I say, "Maybe from the way the guys talk about you."

Unfazed, she shrugs and walks farther into the room. She sits down next to me and gets her supplies out. "I expect it now. There aren't as many women in this field of work anymore. I hope you don't mind me having an assistant today?"

I shake my head as I notice a man enter the room and stand beside her. "What do you want me to do?" he asks.

The woman looks up at him with a smile. "If you could apply the numbing gel on her back and both hands, that would be great." She looks back at me and asks, "Do you mind? He's my husband, by the way. Well, one of them." She gives me a wink and gets back to what she's doing.

The man grabs a tube and comes up to my other side. He smiles down at me and says, "My name's Knox, by the way." He points to his wife. "I'm assuming she didn't introduce herself?"

I shake my head. "No."

He grins as he snaps on a pair of gloves. "She tends to do that. Her name is Blair. If you can lie facing the back of the chair, I can do your back first. That will allow the gel to saturate your back longer since the tattoo is large. I'll do your hands next. I'll be the one doing the art on your hands while she tattoos your back."

I do as he says. He rubs the gel into my back, and I'm surprised at how warm it is. I was expecting the gel to be cold. It tingles a bit as his hand disappears from my back. I hear a popping noise then he says, "I moved the armrests so you can sit with your hands out in front of you."

Pushing back from the chair so I can see where I need to put my hands, I place them up on the armrests and lie back down. I feel him massage the gel into the tops of my hands.

I feel a muted touch on my back, and Blair asks, "How does that feel?"

"I don't feel much."

She hums. "Alright, I'm going to start. If it feels uncomfortable, let me know."

I hum in acknowledgment; then something marks across my back for a few minutes before it stops. I hear the buzz of the machine and know the moment she starts because there's a slight tickle where the needle digs into my skin. Well fuck, this gel shit is fantastic.

I also feel the mark across the top of my hands before another machine's buzz starts. The hand he begins with gives off a slight twinge of pain, but it's not as bad as it would have been without the gel.

With the steady buzz of the machines in the background, I close my eyes and feel myself relax. I don't remember much after that.

Chapter Twenty-Three

JANE

I startle awake when someone touches my shoulder. "What!? What? Where am I?"

Howe snorts and says, "You fell asleep while they were doing your tattoo."

I arch a brow. "Really?" I look around the room to find it's just my guys and me in here. Looking down at my hands, I now have an Asphodelus flower on one hand and a Narcissus flower on the other. Getting up from the chair, I move toward the floor-length mirror in the corner. I turn and look over my shoulder to see my largest tattoo. The Goddess herself. She looks beautiful, surrounded by flowers, but what makes me smirk is the skull she is holding. She's wearing a crown of flowers, but behind them sit black spikes as if to show that she's not only the Goddess of Spring but also the Queen of the Underworld. I fucking love it!

I turn to grin at my guys. "It's beautiful. I love them all."

Jace nods. "She did a great job." He holds out a hand, and I take it as he ushers me out of the shop.

As soon as we step outside, I realize I should have put my bulletproof vest back on. Because while we were busy, the gang we're fighting against dared to enter the Underworld-heavy territory after all.

I'm immediately shoved to the ground and covered by someone's body. Fucking hell! I just got new tattoos! It's a good thing they are covered. From my prone position, I try to get a look at what's going on. Jace still covers me, but I hiss, "Don't fucking worry about me. Go deal with these fuckers!"

He looks down at me, and there must be something in my eyes because he nods and orders, "Stay on the ground." Then he jumps up and pulls out a handgun I didn't even know he had on him.

From my vantage point, I look around to see what's happening. Zane is fighting off a few men but easily takes them out. I look over to find Howe as he pops off shots, hitting his mark each time.

Seeing that the other guys are okay, I frantically look around to find Alec. I find him shooting at our enemies, but then I hear him grunt. As I watch, blood sprays across his arm. Fuck, a bullet grazed him! He shoots off a few more rounds before another shot rings out, and he falls to the ground.

I'm trying not to panic because I know the guys were wearing their bulletproof vests when we left the house. I hear a very un-human growl and look toward the sound. I'm shocked to find Howe on a full rampage.

Holy fucking shit. If I was on the other end of that growl and pure rage . . . I would shit myself. No joke.

Alec lets out a groan as he rolls onto his belly. Howe doesn't pay him any attention, though. He's busy cutting down and shooting anyone in his path. I look around to find that there aren't any enemies left. Howe . . . killed them all. Holy shit.

My eyes widen as he turns around. He's standing there panting, completely covered in blood. He takes in his surroundings for just a moment before he looks down at Alec. As if just now realizing that Alec is fine, his eyes widen. "Fucking hell, Alec! You scared the shit out of me."

I stand from my position and walk over to them as my racing heart begins to slow.

Alec laughs, then groans, "It fucking hurt like a bitch and knocked the wind out of me."

Howe puts away his weapons before holding out a hand to help him up. "Are you sure you're okay?" he asks.

Alec rubs at the spot he was hit, not taking off the vest just yet. "I'm sure I'll have a large bruise."

Jace runs over to us and yells, "Stop talking and get into the fucking car!"

No arguments here. We all hustle into the car. The car is silent as Alpha and Beta drive us back to the house. Once home, we exit the car as a unit and don't divide up until we get inside.

Jace growls as he stomps his way up the stairs. I point in the direction he went and ask, "Where is he going?"

Zane huffs out a sigh but follows Jace up the stairs. "He's going to the office to come up with a plan." He pauses, looks down at us, and says, "I'm going to try to help out. Howe, you definitely need a shower. Jane can help put some of that bruise balm on Alec's chest."

Zane skips a few steps as he makes his way down the hallway to help Jace. I look over to my other boys and smile. "Well, you heard the man. Let's go."

We settle into what I assume is Howe's room. Alec takes off his shirt and vest, hissing in the process. My nose scrunches up at the darkening bruise on his chest.

Alec laughs. "That bad?"

I scoop out a glob of bruise balm and rub it over the ever-expanding area. "It will definitely bruise even with the balm."

Alec just shrugs and says, "I've had worse." Once I'm done applying the balm to his chest, he stretches out on the bed and closes his eyes. It doesn't take long before his soft snores fill the quiet room.

Howe exits the bathroom in a cloud of steam. He looks over to see Alec snoring and smiles. He saunters over to the bed to snuggle up to Alec. I watch as he runs his fingers softly through Alec's hair, almost as if reassuring himself that Alec is okay.

"Can I ask you a question?"

Howe shifts his gaze over to me and says, "Sure."

I point between him and Alec. "How did this all start?"

He smirks. "Well, to explain how our relationship started, I would have to tell you about the day he killed Foster Fuck."

"Foster Fuck?" I repeat, a little confused.

Howe frowns. "Our Foster dad."

I nod. I remember them saying that the guy was a total asshole. He was also a child fucker, so I don't really feel bad that the guy is gone. Making myself comfortable on the bed, I say, "I'm all ears."

His gaze shifts back to Alec as he continues playing with his hair. "So about nine years ago or so . . ."

Chapter Twenty-Four

HOWE

About nine years ago . . .

I watch as Alec paces the room. He's been fighting himself for so long, and I don't think he even realizes he's doing it. I saw his face when we walked by the quarterback at school. He had a slight blush on his cheeks. I know he thinks guys are just as cute as girls, and I have no issue with it. I'm a man who thinks everyone has the potential to be attractive. I know they have a fancy name for it, but it's just easier to tell people I'm bisexual.

I look for a person's soul. Their personality. If I am honest with myself, I have a huge fucking crush on Alec. He's fucking sexy, don't get me wrong. But he has a great personality too. And his soul. Fuck. His soul is fucking beautiful.

"I'm going to kill him, Howe," Alec grits out as he paces the room.

"Then kill him."

His surprised gaze flicks to mine. "Are you serious?"

I shrug and say, "Why the fuck not. It's not like anyone would miss the fuck."

He throws his hands in the air. "I can't kill the man by myself! He's fucking huge if you haven't noticed."

I roll my eyes. "I know the fucker is huge, but so am I."

He snorts. "So you're offering to help me kill him?"

"Of course, I would fucking help you." Then I whisper, "I would do anything for you."

He looks at me for a moment as if to gauge if I'm serious or not. Something about my face must tell him I'm serious. He huffs. "It's not like I can just go up to him and kill him. We should talk to Jace and Zane about this too."

I shake my head and tell him, "They won't give a fuck. No one has more reason to kill that fucker than you do." I jump up from my spot on the bed. Grabbing my hunting knife, I hold it in the air and say, "Let's go."

"You're . . . you're not serious, are you?"

I smirk over my shoulder at him as I open the bedroom door. "As serious as a heart attack. Let's go kill us a child fucker, Love." I can't help the swell of satisfaction I feel when his cheeks flush pink from the endearment. I only use it when no one else is around. I respect his boundaries, but I want him to know that I see him. I see him and don't care.

Alec follows me as we make our way down the stairs. I know exactly where the Foster Fuck will be. I turn the corner to find that he's sitting in his recliner, dead fucking asleep from drinking too much. Perfect. Handing the knife to Alec behind me, I waste no time making my way over to the man of the hour. I'm bigger than I used to be, and I certainly outweigh him now, so when I rip him off the recliner and put him in a headlock, he doesn't fight. He's too fucking drunk to fight back.

"What the hell are you two asswipes doing? Get the hell off me, you delinquent!" He screams as I pull him out the door and into the backyard. I drag him into the wood shop. Once I'm in the middle of the shop, I switch up my hold. I lock my arms under his armpits and brace my hands behind his head. He's still screaming, but I ignore him.

Looking over, I see Alec standing right in front of me. His eyes are wide, and his hands shake as he holds the hunting knife. I give him a smirk to reassure him that everything is alright. Speaking in a low, calm voice, I say, "I have him. He can't hurt you. Never again. It's your turn to hurt him now, Alec."

Foster Fuck snorts and stupidly spits out, "Like you kids could really hurt me. What are you going to do with that knife? Nothing. Absolutely nothing. You're pathetic."

I see the switch flip in Alec; the moment something shifts in his head. He unsheathes the knife and slowly walks toward us. His eyes meet mine for just a moment as if asking for permission to seek this justice. I give him a nod.

Without hesitation, he slams the knife into Foster Fuck's chest. Then he pulls it out and stabs downward into Foster Fuck's crotch. Foster Fuck screams, but no one can hear him. No one but us.

Alec removes the knife, stabbing his chest again, and again, and again. My heart clenches when I see tears gather in Alec's eyes as he continues stabbing this fucker. Blood speckles across his cheeks, and the tears fall. Alec screams, "This is for every fucking touch I said I didn't want!" He stabs again. "This is for ruining every sexual relationship I'll ever have!" He stabs Foster Fuck one last time and leaves the knife in as he whispers, "For ruining the beauty of finding a man attractive."

I let Foster Fuck slip through my grasp. He crumbles to the floor, but I only have eyes for Alec. My precious Alec. Should blood look so fucking sexy on a person? Maybe it has to be the right person. Alec looks up at me, and I see it. The ghost that has been haunting him for so long is now dead.

I can't stop myself from reaching out and cupping his cheek. His eyes flutter closed for a moment before opening again. My grin is wide as I say, "That was fucking epic. Not to mention hot as hell."

He sputters out a laugh. "I'm not sure that being covered in blood and having a mental breakdown should be considered hot."

I snicker as I say, "Well when it's you, it is."

He looks down at himself and winces. "I should probably get cleaned up. What do we do about him?"

I wave off his concern. "I already texted Jace. He's on it. But I do have a question for you."

He arches a brow. "Um . . . okay."

My heart flutters, and suddenly I'm nervous as fuck. Holy shit. Rubbing the back of my head, I ask, "Would you mind going out to dinner with me tonight? We could go to the arcades you like."

His brows scrunch together as he says, "Um . . . I guess so. But you know Jace and Zane hate the arcades."

Palming my face, I say through a groan, "It would just be you and me."

His eyes widen. "You and me?"

"Yeah. Like . . . you know . . . a date," I mumble. Holy fuck, that wasn't smooth at all.

"You . . . you want to go on a date with me?" Alec squeaks out.

I shrug, trying to play it cool as I admit, "Well yeah . . . I mean . . . I've had the biggest crush on you for like ever so . . ." I pause and look up at his face to find it bright red. "I mean . . . if you don't want to . . ."

"NO!" he squeals loudly, then waves his hands around. "Wait! No! That wasn't what I meant! I mean . . . shit!"

I can't help but smile at how flustered he is. "So . . . is that a yes to the date?"

He nods enthusiastically. "Yes!" Then he looks down at himself again. "But I need to get cute first!" He runs out of the workshop without a second glance back. I look down at the man who has haunted us for so long. "I hope you're burning wherever the fuck you are."

Without a backward glance, knowing my brothers will handle this mess, I make my way back to the house to get ready myself. I have a date tonight. A date with a guy I've had a crush on for years. Best. Night. Ever.

Four years later . . .

We've been secretly dating for four years now. We didn't mean for the secret to go on for this long, but every time Alec and I thought about telling Jace and Zane, we chickened out. But today is the day. We need to tell them.

I squeeze Alec's hand in silent support as we walk down the dark hallway of our new house. I am not sure how Jace managed to get this mansion-like house, but I think it has something to do with the number of gangs we've taken over. The cave we use for our compound belonged to one of those gangs. We took it as payment for our protection, so I assume this mansion was the same.

Hand in hand, we walk down the hallway toward the living room where the others are. Jace is hovering over a computer typing, and Zane is sharpening his newest set of knives. Fucking weirdo. I swear the man would buy a scythe if he could.

I clear my throat to get their attention. They both look up from what they're doing. Somehow in sync, they both look down at my hand in Alec's, then back up at our faces. Without a single word, they continue with what they were doing a moment ago.

Furrowing my brows, I clear my throat again. They both look up again, and Jace arches a brow as if saying, "Get on with it."

Huffing out a breath, I say, "Alec and I would like to tell you something." It's Zane who raises a brow this time.

"Howe and I have been in a secret relationship for the last four years," Alec blurts out rapidly. He doesn't even take a breath.

I look over at him with my brow arched this time and mouth, "Seriously?"

He whines and apologizes. "Sorry."

I squeeze his hand in reassurance, then look back at the two men I have considered brothers since I was brought to that horrible foster house. Zane and Jace exchange glances, and then Zane shrugs. Just . . . shrugs and goes back to sharpening his knives.

Slightly confused by the reaction, I look at Jace and arch a brow. Jace shrugs before he says, "I don't care who you fuck. Well, I'm assuming there's fucking but whatever. I also don't care who you love as long as you're fucking happy."

My mouth gapes open. What. The. Fuck. I was expecting . . . well, to be honest, I wasn't sure what to expect, but it wasn't that.

Alec's voice is surprisingly high pitched as he says, "Wait, wait, wait! We freaked out for three weeks for that reaction?" Alec points at Jace and demands, "I need a better reaction!" Then pointing to Zane, he says, "You too!"

Zane looks back up in confusion and asks, "Were you hoping I'd be disgusted?" Then, in a monotone voice, he says, "How could you? Oh. The horror. The horror."

In the same monotone voice. Jace adds, "Our best friends. No. Oh, no. How dare you." Zane and Jace look at each other and begin laughing their asses off.

Alec looks at me, and without meaning to, we say in unison, "Assholes!" But there isn't much heat behind it, considering we are both smiling like loons.

That seems to set Zane and Jace off even more. They now have tears streaming down their faces from laughing so hard. But I have to admit, I've never been happier seeing my brothers laugh. It's been so long since I've heard them laugh. I haven't seen them smile in a long time, either.

I can't stop myself as I begin to chuckle. Their laughter is infectious.

Chapter Twenty-Five

JANE

I can't stop the giggle that erupts from my lips. That sounds like a reaction Jace and Zane would have. I cover my mouth to try to subdue the giggle, but it doesn't work.

Howe looks up at me with a grin. "Seriously?"

"It seems like a very Jace and Zane thing to do to tease you about their reactions. Did you really think they would hate you because of your feelings?"

He shrugs, but he's got a light blush on his cheeks. "At the time, it seemed like a big deal. I respect the shit out of them, and I didn't want anything to change. I didn't want them to look at me differently."

I move over to snuggle up against his side as he continues playing with Alec's hair. Laying my head against his shoulder, I say, "You guys have been through too much together for something like who you love to break you apart."

Howe sighs and replies, "Foster Fuck really messed with Alec's head as far as relationships go. I'm not going to lie; I was a bit fucked up too. I didn't want the only people I've ever cared about to see me the way Foster Fuck did."

"I highly doubt Jace and Zane would ever look at you like the Foster Fuck did. I also don't believe they would ever stop loving you just because you like guys."

He hums thoughtfully. "Hetero guys just seem to get weird when they find out that you like guys. Like suddenly, you must find them attractive and want to fuck them. I didn't want Jace and Zane to react the same way."

I snort out a laugh. "I feel like that's the norm. They are the same way with women. They thought that because I was a stripper, that meant I wanted their dick. Like seriously, I have standards. And you being an overbearing asshole is low as far as standards go. No thanks."

Howe snorts. "True." He shifts down the bed a bit to cuddle Alec and me, then kisses my forehead before saying, "You should probably go take a quick shower too."

I look down at myself and realize that my black dress has a few tears from being shoved to the ground. I also have a few scrapes on my knees and palms from the gravel digging into my skin. Pushing myself up, I briefly press my lips against his before pulling away. "You're probably right. I'll be back soon."

By the time I'm done with my shower and enter the bedroom, Howe is cuddled up to Alec, snoring softly. I look around the room in search of one of their shirts to wear. Finding one, I slip it on. I'm not about to walk naked to my bedroom to grab underwear. Looking back to the bed to see my two boys, I shrug, deciding to just slip into the bed the way I am.

Smirking, I wiggle onto the bed in between Howe and Alec. Alec's breathing changes as he flips to snuggle my front, and Howe shifts backward a bit so I can fit between them. Howe snuggles his front to my back as he wraps his arm around Alec and me. Their smoky and leathery scents surround me, and I breathe deeply, letting it calm me. Their familiar scents make me feel safe, and my body relaxes as darkness rises to greet me.

Sometime later, I wake up feeling a hard body pressed against my front and an extremely hard bulge against my ass. Warm breath whispers against my neck. Howe seems to be still asleep. Slowly opening my eyes, I'm greeted with a smile and a pair of honey-golden eyes staring at me. Alec's silver hair is tousled from sleep. He smirks as he says, "Good morning, Moonbeam." His voice is still rough from sleep. Fucking sexy.

Caressing his cheek, I smile. "Good morning, Alec. Did you sleep well?"

Leaning forward, he presses his lips lightly against mine. He pulls away enough so that our lips are barely touching as he whispers, "I had an amazing night with my two favorite people."

I grin against his lips. "Me too," I whisper back.

He pulls away, looking behind me. His eyes meet mine again, and I see mischief sparking behind them. "Do you want to play a game?"

Arching a brow, I respond, "Depends on the game."

"You want to help me wake Howe up?"

I giggle, and because I'm always up for a game with these guys, I ask, "What do you have in mind?"

Alec grins as he pulls away. He turns on the lamp beside the bed, which bathes the room in a warm, soft glow. He crooks his finger in a "come here" motion, and I slowly slip away from Howe so as not to wake him. I turn to look down at a sleeping Howe, and Alec stands behind me. His light-chocolate skin glows under the lamplight, and his long, black curls lay in disarray on his head. I am not usually a girl who likes facial hair, but Howe's short goatee is sexy as fuck.

Alec grabs me and wraps me in his arms. He kisses my neck and whispers, "I was thinking I could get you nice and ready." He slides one hand up my thigh and one under my shirt. Fuck! I forgot I was completely naked under this shirt. His fingers whisper over my lower abdomen, sending goose bumps over my skin. I suck in a breath as he continues his exploration lower. "I could get you nice and wet. Then you could wake him with your pussy wrapped around his cock."

I moan as he slips his fingers between my folds. I know I'm already wet from just his words. His other hand slips under my shirt and massages my breasts as he caresses my clit. I groan, and Alec snickers behind me. Howe shifts a bit in his sleep before settling again, so Alec nips at my ear and whispers, "You have to be quiet, or you'll wake him too early."

I nod and bite my lip to keep my sounds of pleasure at bay. Alec slips one finger inside me, pumping slowly. I raise my arms and wrap them around his neck behind me. Sliding my fingers into his hair, I tug. He grunts and slips another finger inside me. I bite harder on my lip as I try to push myself deeper onto his fingers. Fuck! I need him to go faster.

I turn my head enough so that I can pull his face down to mine and devour his mouth. He groans as he slips another finger inside, fucking me with his fingers now. He moves faster as I deepen the kiss. His grip on my breast tightens, and I can't help but rub my ass against his hard cock.

He moves his hand in such a way that he can rub my clit at the same time his fingers thrust faster inside me. Feeling myself tighten around his fingers, I bite his lower lip to stop from screaming as I come on his fingers.

He thrusts his cock against my ass and lets out a low groan. Slowly, he pulls his fingers from my dripping pussy. My eyes flutter open, and I look to find his open wide. I'm confused for a moment until I feel the wetness on my ass. Did . . . did he just come in his underwear? From finger fucking me? I grin up at him because, holy shit, does that make my ego soar.

He must see the amusement in my eyes because he growls and pulls away. He smacks my ass and orders, "Go fuck our man and wake him up."

I can't help my grin as he slips off the bed, removing his now-damp underwear. "I'm sure he would enjoy both of us waking him."

Alec arches a brow at me, then shrugs and climbs back onto the bed. I move over to Howe gently so I don't jostle the bed too much. He's lying on his back, which allows me to slide his boxers down his body slowly. I slip them down just far enough that his hard cock pops out, but I don't remove them.

Still wet from my orgasm, I position myself over him. Alec grins as he comes up next to me and holds Howe's cock in position, so I can lazily slide down his length. Howe groans as his eyes flutter open. His hands slide up my thighs till they rest on my hips. His voice is deep and gravelly from sleep as he says, "Fucking hell! This is an amazing way to wake up."

Once I'm fully seated on his cock, I moan at how full I feel. Gradually, I begin to rise and fall on his dick as his grip on my hips tightens. I can tell he is trying not to thrust up each time, letting me set the pace. Alec moves over to capture Howe's lips with his, and I slam myself down on Howe's cock with a moan. Fuck, they look sexy kissing each other like that. Howe slips one of his hands off my hips and into Alec's hair, gripping hard as he growls into Alec's mouth. Howe seems to attack Alec's mouth as he gives up the fight of not thrusting. He thrusts up each time I lower back down.

I'm panting as I chase my orgasm. It's so close. Suddenly, I feel a hand between my legs. I open my eyes, not realizing I had closed them. Alec starts rubbing my clit as he continues to ravage Howe's mouth. My orgasm hits, and I scream. Howe pushes Alec away with a loud growl and returns his other hand to my hip as he thrusts upward forcefully with a roar.

Heaving breaths leave him as he gives me a wicked smile. He looks over to Alec, then back up at me before announcing, "My turn."

I'm slightly confused when he quickly flips me over. My back is now against the bed, and he slowly pulls out. I whine at the loss of the fullness I previously felt. Looking down at me, he asks, "Do you mind if Alec fucks you while I enjoy the view this time?"

I grin up at Howe and look over at Alec. I can't help but tease him. "You want to come inside me this time instead of in your underwear?"

His eyes blaze as he moves between my legs. "You're going to pay for that, Jane."

I smirk up at him. "Am I?"

Without warning, he sheathes himself to the hilt. I'm still soaked, so it isn't painful, but fuck! I hiss out a breath as he grunts. He begins thrusting slowly, and I growl in irritation. Alec doesn't get a chance to say anything before Howe is beside us, smashing his lips to Alec's. Howe tweaks each of my nipples with one hand, but his other isn't in view.

Alec has one hand on my hip and the other twined in Howe's dark curls. I hear Alec growl, then suddenly slam into me. I can't stop myself from blabbering, "Yes . . . fucking fuck me damnit."

I notice Howe smirking against Alec's lips and look down to find Howe wiping the slickness off of his cock from our combined release. As I watch, he slips his hand behind Alec, and I wonder what he's doing. Alec pulls away from Howe's lips with a whine, then hovers over me.

Alec's thrusts slow due to whatever Howe is doing, and I hiss in frustration. Faster damnit!

Howe smirks, and as if reading my mind, he says, "You better fuck our woman the way she wants to be fucked, or I'll stop."

Alec shakes his head as he pants out, "Don't stop." Then Alec's lips are suddenly on mine, and he slams his cock into me the way I want. He whimpers into my mouth and wiggles his ass, which makes his cock do the same inside me. That's when I realize Howe is fucking his ass with his fingers while Alec fucks me.

Somehow, Howe manages to slide his other hand between Alec and me to play with my clit as he fucks Alec's ass with his fingers. Howe must hit the right spot because suddenly, Alec is slamming into me while moaning into my mouth. As he slowly thrusts through his orgasm, I feel his hot seed fill me.

"Don't you fucking dare stop fucking our girl until she comes too. You don't leave our woman unsatisfied," Howe growls and pinches my clit.

Between Howe pinching my clit and Alec slamming against just the right spot, I come again. It's not as mind-blowing as the other orgasms, but fucking amazing nonetheless. I lie there panting as Howe pecks Alec on the cheek, then looks down at me with a grin. He slides closer to me, pressing his lips softly against mine.

He pulls away with a smile and says, "Love you, Starlight."

I smile up at him and say, "I love you, too." My eyes shift to Alec, and I say, "I love you too, Alec."

Chapter Twenty-Six

JANE

It's been a few weeks since the incident with Alec getting shot. My tattoos are healing nicely, and they look amazing. I keep asking the guys if I can get my facial tattoo, but they said that they want to lie low for a while because of what happened the last time we were at the shop.

Although it's been quiet the last few weeks, I feel like something big is going to happen soon. I've enjoyed fucking with Jace over the last few weeks, though. Messing with him when he gives me orders and giving him way more attitude than necessary.

I grin to myself; it makes for great sex with him. Which is why I keep doing it. I give him attitude, and he teaches me a lesson on why I shouldn't give Hades attitude. As Persephone, I don't mind the lessons. I don't mind them as Jane either, but my attitude seems to irritate him more when he's acting as Hades.

I make my way to the meeting room before we have our session with the people of our territory. I'm in my complete Persephone outfit, along with my face paint. I'm getting a bit better with the paint, but I still make Jax do it. He still does it better than I can.

Speaking of Jax, he and Silas are trailing behind me as Alpha and Beta, my personal bodyguards. My heels click across the floor as I let out a sigh.

Jax speeds up to walk next to me. He bumps my shoulder and asks, "What's wrong, Seph?"

I shrug and try to explain, "I feel like something bad is going to happen today. The gang has been too quiet since the attack a few weeks ago. I feel like they would have attacked again after what happened with Charon."

Jax nods. "It is odd that they haven't attacked again."

Silas comes up next to me. He grunts and then says, "Nothing will happen to you while on our watch."

I hum. "It's not me that I'm worried about."

Jax bumps my shoulder again. "You are the one who they are going to come after. You are Hades' weakness."

Nodding, I say, "I suppose you're right." My new shadows follow me into the room for our meeting. They are right. I am the weak point for all of the males in this room. If the enemy got to me, I'm sure the guys would do anything and everything to get me back. Even if I didn't want them to.

I groan as I leave the meeting room. Jace wanted to have a meeting after talking to and giving away favors to the people of our territory. Stupid meetings. With a wave to Silas, I make my way down the hallway toward the bedroom area of the cave. I know he will follow behind soon to guard my door. I am sure Jax will be there soon too. I would rather be heading to the house, but the guys don't want me there without them and security. So I'm stuck here until they are done. As much as it irritates me, I can understand it. With my father now sending people out to find and capture me, plus the enemies of the Underworld hot on our asses, I can understand them wanting me close.

That didn't stop me from arguing with Jace for an hour, though. I grin, thinking about his face. He was made to be Hades. Fire lit in his eyes every time we fought. Huffing out a breath, I close my bedroom door behind me. Silas and Jax won't come in, but that will not stop my guys. I also lock the bathroom door behind me, not wanting the guys to sneak in while I'm showering. They love to do that. I grin, looking at myself in the mirror. I touch the delicate-looking feathers in my hair. The barrette looks like a hair accessory but holds three knives within its sheath. Howe smiles every time he sees it. I never leave the house or compound without it.

I leave it in, not planning on washing my hair, and jump in the shower. Scrubbing quickly, I wash my body and jump out. I wrap myself in a towel and make my way over to the mirror. Wiping away the fog, I notice something odd in the reflection over my shoulder. But before I can look behind me, I feel a hand around my mouth and a sharp pain in my abdomen.

Looking back up and into the mirror, I find a masked man standing behind me and a knife protruding from my lower abdomen. How the fuck did this guy get past Silas and Jax?! Fuck! Shit! Okay, think Jane. I need to get away from him. Ah fuck, this is going to hurt like a bitch! Taking as deep a breath as I can with my mouth and nose covered, I stomp down on his foot as hard as possible. He lets out a grunt, and his grip loosens on my face so that I can pull myself forward enough to ram my head back into his face. Finally, he releases my face, and that's when I pull one of the knives out of my hair. Turning as quickly as I can, I slash it across his throat. I grin at the triumph I feel, realizing I just killed this mother fucker. But I also realize that he pulled the knife out of my abdomen as I twisted.

Looking down, I see that most of my towel is red, and I'm dripping blood all over the floor. "Well, fuck!" I watch as the guy tries his damndest to staunch the bleeding from his neck, but it won't work. My knives are sharp and could slice through an abdomen like butter. I watch him brace himself against the bathroom door and slide down to the floor, leaving a red trail behind him like a slug. When I realize he is blocking the door, I groan. Fuck! FUCK! I look around the room, trying to remember where I put my phone. Fucking shit! I left it out in the bedroom. Feeling myself getting dizzy, I slide to the floor in front of the sink. I reach up to grab another towel and shove it against the wound, hoping to slow the blood flow long enough for someone to find me.

With all the energy I have left, I scream as loud as I can, "FUCK! HELP!"

Then I collapse into darkness.

Jace

I watch Jane leave the room in a huff. I swear that woman frustrates me and causes fights just to rile me up.

"You realize she only fights with you to get a reaction, right, brother?"

I roll my eyes. It's like he can read my mind. "Yes, Thanatos. I realize our Persephone loves to do it just to frustrate me." I hear the others laugh. When we finish the plans to get our entire territory under control and find out how our enemies are getting inside information, we are going hunting. I know Jane wants her freedom, but the town isn't safe with her father looking for her and our enemies finding ways to get to us. The sound of hurried boots across the floor has me looking up. Silas enters the room out of breath. Quickly, I rise from my chair. "What is it, Alpha?"

He pants and explains, "I heard screaming from Persephone's room, Hades. I ran all the way here due to her being in her bathroom. The bathroom door is locked, and Beta is trying to get a response so he can enter. I have Hounds guarding the area, but I knew you would want to be there." I wanted to scream at him and ask why he didn't just call. But I know that the reception is shit down here. We need to get better radios.

I nod, trying to contain my rage. "Let's go then." I take off, running toward her room as my brothers follow behind. I approach the Hounds guarding her room and nod when they bow slightly in greeting. "When did you hear the scream?"

One of the Hounds looks at his watch. "About five minutes ago, Hades. We rushed to find you as soon as we could."

I nod, understanding that it isn't his fault we have unreliable equipment. That is going to change. Rushing into the room, I see Beta banging on the door with panic as he screams, "Seph, answer the fucking door!"

I slide up beside him and bang on the door before calling out, "I'm coming in, Seph." There's no response. I was hoping to get a response like I always do. I bang on the door again. "Seph! You need to talk to me, Princess." I know calling her that pisses her off. I wait for her answer. Nothing. "Persephone, answer the fucking door, or I'm kicking it down!" I was so close to calling her name but thought better of it. We never use our names at the compound unless it is in a whisper or in a secure room. With good reason. Only our Underworld names. "Fuck it. I'm coming in, Seph!" I kick the door and hit a bit of resistance. Turning to Howe, I point at the door. "Destroy, Cerberus!" He grins, but it doesn't reach his eyes, and he nods, backing up a bit. Then, going full force, he runs right through the door, splitting it in half. I watch as he trips over a body.

"Fuck!" he yells as he falls into a pool of blood. A fuck ton of blood.

I rush through the door and see the person he tripped over is a mask-covered man. I ignore him knowing my brothers will figure out who he is soon enough. Searching the room for Jane, I find her slumped against the sink with a towel pressed against her abdomen. She's pale as fuck. I rush over to her and check for a pulse. I huff out a breath in relief. It's faint, but a pulse is a pulse. Looking over my shoulder, I shout, "Alpha!" I see Beta helping the others with the unidentified man but watch as his eyes drift over to Jane. They are filled with panic at the amount of blood surrounding us.

Alpha rushes into the room and gasps when he sees Jane. His eyes meet mine, and there's true panic. Seems our Jane has captured the loyalty of my Hellhounds. Not only as Persephone but as Jane too. He shakes himself, and determination blazes in his eyes as he asks, "What do you need, Hades?"

"Search the compound for anything that looks out of the ordinary. Have Beta call the doctor to come immediately!" Glancing back down at my girl, I say, "Also, have him bring blood and an assistant." I look back over my shoulder to make sure my orders are obeyed. He nods and runs off. I run my fingers over her pale face and pull the towel away to assess the damage.

The towel wrapped around her is stained dark red with blood, so I push the towel in my hand harder against the fresh blood. She lets out a grunt.

"Hey, Princess. It's okay. We are here now. You hold on for me, okay?" I watch as her eyes flutter open. Her once bright gray-blue eyes look dull. Hands cover mine, and I lift my head to find Zane. He nods at me, and I release the towel. Without realizing it, I place the bloodied hand I had against her wound on her cheek. "Keep your eyes on me, okay?"

"I'll be fine. Just tired," she whispers. I watch as her eyes slowly dull even more. No! Fuck, no! I won't survive losing her again.

"Seph! You need to keep your eyes open," I beg as I press my forehead to hers. "You need to hold on," I whisper, "Please don't leave us." I pull away, hoping her eyes will be on me. But I'm greeted with nothing except her shallow breaths. I hear rustling and shouting behind me before Beta comes back into the room.

He's panting as he says, "He's here! The doctor is already in the operating room. I have the path guarded and cleared for you, sir."

Can't really call it an operating room; it's more like a makeshift hospital for any of our men who get shot or sliced open. It wasn't meant for major surgery, but we can't chance a hospital right now. My eyes meet Beta's, and I see the worry in his eyes. Fuck, I can't thank these two men enough. I knew the moment I saw them all those years ago that they would never betray us. They are part of the family. I nod and lift Jane as carefully as I can. I settle her against me so that the towel pushes against her abdomen with my own. Then I run. I run as fast as I can. I will not lose this woman. I can't.

All I can do is watch as the assistant and the doctor rush her away on the silver gurney I placed her on. Looking down at myself, I realize I am soaked in red. Drenched in her blood. My brothers come up beside me, and I have a déjà vu moment. It's like a flashback to when we were young and couldn't do anything but watch as she was taken away from us. The only difference is we may not get her back this time. For the first time in all the years I have been Hades, I pray to a God I don't believe in. I pray to anyone who will hear my plea. "Please don't take her from us."

Zane starts humming softly beside me. I listen closely and realize it's a song I haven't heard him hum in years. *You are my sunshine.* He would hum that song for her when she was upset. I suppose I couldn't fault him for not humming it in so long. For years, I couldn't play a song on the piano.

I hear him whisper, "Please don't take my Sunshine away."

I have to admit; the song embodies their relationship. Not only is his nickname for her Sunshine, but she was his Sunshine. The part where the girl leaves and loves another isn't true. But she did leave, and it shattered all of his dreams. I had never seen my brother fall into darkness so completely until that day. I feel a hand on my shoulder and look to my right, finding Alec.

"The Gods won't take her from us," he says with all the confidence I wish I had right now.

"How do you figure?" Zane asks to my left.

Alec grins. It looks like the grin he gives to the guilty people we kill. Devilish and full of evil intent. "Because they fear the demons we would become without her."

I laugh. It sounds a bit rough, but he's right, though. We would tear this world apart without her. I nod as I continue starting toward the spot they took her away. "Then we wait. We wait to hear if the gates of the Underworld open. If they do . . . we take every soul from this world as we follow behind her."

Chapter Twenty-Seven

JANE

I groan when my brain decides it's time to wake up. My body? Yeah, it doesn't agree. Fuck, my side hurts. I feel like I've been hit by a Mack truck. Lifting a hand to rub at my eyes, I moan at the amount of effort it takes. Damn, I feel weak. I hear a rustling beside me. Squinting, I open my eyes to gauge the brightness. I sigh when I see that the room is softly lit.

Turning toward the noise, I find Zane sitting on a chair. He looks extremely uncomfortable, in my opinion. His head rests at an awkward angle, and his arms are crossed over his chest. I watch him blink a few times before his eyes meet mine. I must have woken him up.

He immediately jumps up from the chair when he notices I'm awake. "Hey! You're finally awake."

I look around the room to find that he's the only one here, and I'm on my bed. Odd place to be. Zane notes my confused expression and hurries to explain.

"You were resting in our makeshift med bay for a few hours to make sure you were stable, but we thought you would be more comfortable up here in your own bed." He points to the red bag hanging on the IV pole and adds, "You're on your last bag of blood. They had to give you a transfusion. You lost a lot, but the doc said your blood values are improving."

I give him a weak nod before asking, "Where are the others?"

He rubs the back of his neck. "We've been up for hours. I kicked them out so they could get some sleep. I told them I would wake them if anything changed."

I smirk. "They actually left?"

He shrugs. "I mentioned that I kicked them out, right? They were hovering and stressing out. I told them their constant stomping around the room would wake you."

I huff out a laugh and instantly regret it. Fucking hell, that hurt. Zane tenses when he notices my wince of pain, but I wave a hand in the air and tell him, "I'm fine."

He snorts out a laugh. "You are not fine, Sunshine. I better go get the others."

"Wait," I hiss as I adjust a bit on the bed, trying to find a more comfortable position. "Let them sleep a little longer. Come sit with me." He debates my words for a moment before sitting back down on the chair. Sighing, I say, "I'm not made of porcelain. Come sit on the bed."

He looks like he will refuse but acquiesces with my wishes. He shifts onto the mattress softly to avoid jostling the bed too much. He's close enough that I can shift and put my head in his lap.

I grin. "A much better pillow."

He doesn't laugh, but I can hear it in his voice as he says, "As long as you're comfortable." He begins running his fingers through my hair and sighs as I relax into his touch. We sit in silence for a moment before he starts humming.

I love when he hums. My mind drifts, and I start thinking about the new scar that will be added to my collection. That reminds me of the scar on Zane's face. I never really think much about it; it's not the first thing I notice. "Hey Zane, can I ask you something?"

"Depends," he jokes.

I slap his thigh softly. "Ha ha, funny. Anyways, I was wondering if you would tell me how you got your scar?"

His fingers pause in my hair. "You want to know how I got my scar? Right now?"

I shrug. "I have nothing better to do. I am curious about it but haven't found the right time to ask."

He hums. "I guess so. Well, it happened when we were eighteen."

Zane

About five years ago . . .

Fucking hell. This new gang is going to be a bitch to deal with. I had told Jace that this one was going to be a problem. They have been fighting us for the last few years. They are the only ones who we haven't been able to get under our control. The only one to not fall into line.

Huffing out a sigh, I look around our new headquarters. We were finally able to "acquire" the cave right outside of town. I say acquire because we took it from one of the other gangs as payment for our protection. At least someone knew who was going to run this territory. We have our fingers in every city now, and the gangs in those cities help us run the Territory of New York. This is the last gang that we need to squash and get under control.

"Are you sure about this, Hades?" I ask as I walk over to Jace, who's still sitting on his Gaudi-looking throne. I didn't really understand why he wanted the thing until I saw him sitting in it the other night with only the black lights on. He'd had on his black suit and looked every bit the part of Hades when he looked up at me. Our black light tattoos have finally healed enough that we could start having meetings with people who wanted our help. His black-out sclera lenses, on top of everything else, made him look like the dark ruler of the Underworld.

He sits there for a moment before sighing and saying, "I don't want to do this, but they have left us no other choice. They will not bow, so at this point, we must break them into submission."

I huff out a sigh. I agree, but that doesn't mean I have to like the idea. "When are we moving out?" As the last word leaves my mouth, Alec and Howe enter the room.

Jace nods toward them. "I was waiting for Cerberus and Charon to get here."

Looking behind me, I find Howe completely covered in black, with several weapons attached to his body. I wouldn't expect anything less from our weapons specialist. I look over to see Alec is in a similar outfit but with his usual handguns rather than knives.

Jace stands from his seat and walks toward the exit. He's also dressed in black, carrying several knives and his handgun.

I groan as I follow behind. I fucking hate having to fight to get this last gang under our control. I have a feeling it is going to be a bloody fight. When we exit the cave, we find the gang waiting for us. Great. That was sarcasm, in case you didn't catch that.

The leader of their group doesn't even give us a moment to take in their numbers before he goes for Jace. He fights the man off easily and takes on the next one who comes at him. I turn to focus on my own fight.

We are down to only a few men when I turn to find one guy sneaking up behind Jace. He doesn't even realize the guy is behind him because he's fighting off another guy. I stab the guy that I'm fighting and race over.

The angle the guy tries to slash Jace is an odd one, and unfortunately, I'm low enough to the ground to stab my knife into the guy's abdomen. Unfortunately, you ask? Well, my face is in the path of his knife, causing it to slash across my left eye. I can't stop the pain-filled scream that I let out. Fuck that hurts! The searing pain from the wound radiates into my skull.

The beat of my heart thumps loudly in my ears, making the pain in my head worse.

The man is on the ground, coughing up blood due to my blow, but he's smiling up at me. I cover my left eye instantly, but it doesn't stop the blood flow.

"Zane!" Jace yells from behind me. Seems he's forgotten to use code names in his frantic state. Can't really blame him, though. He grabs my shoulder and spins me to face him. When my right eye meets his, I see his look of utter devastation. Guess the amount of blood I've lost is worse than I thought. He looks around, and he screams, "Howe! Call the doctor!"

Good thing that the gang who used to own the cave had a small medical bay in the lower part. Jace drags me through the cave entrance as he growls out, "Why the fuck did you do that?"

I snort a laugh, then wince because fuck, that hurt. "Like I was going to let some fucker stab you from behind."

He glares over his shoulder at me as he snaps, "So you used your face to protect me?!"

"Not intentionally. My face just happened to be in the path of his knife. I didn't react fast enough to get my face out of the way. It's not that big of a deal." That is a lie. I know it is a big deal, but I don't need him to blame himself more than he already is.

He shoves me onto the makeshift hospital bed and runs to grab gauze. He thrusts it at me, and I put it in place under my hand. He's still glaring at me, but I can see the worry behind his eyes. "This may cause you to go blind in that eye," he grunts out.

I shrug, trying to act like it doesn't bother me. "Better to be blind than have a dead brother."

He sighs heavily as he collapses onto the chair next to the bed. Bowing his head, he shoves his fingers angrily into his hair. "This isn't how this was supposed to go," he whispers.

Huffing, I place a reassuring hand on his head and ruffle his hair because I know it pisses him off. I smirk when he swats my hand. "You'd think you were brooding over a lover or something," I tease.

He snorts out a laugh. "I love you, brother but not that much."

Glad that I could lighten his mood, I can't help but reply, "I've heard I'm a great fuck."

Jace looks up at me and jokes, "Who said that?" He laughs. "You haven't fucked anyone since that one girl a year or so back. What was her name again? It sounded like a stripper name."

That makes me chuckle, although my head is throbbing. "True enough. Her name was Candy. Short for Candace."

He grins. "That's right. Anyways, I wouldn't take her word for it even if I wanted to fuck you. Which I don't."

"Good. I don't want to fuck you either." I smile. We are silent for a moment before I say, "There are always casualties in war, brother."

"I know," he says with a sigh.

"I, for one, am glad that it's my sight and not your life."

Chapter Twenty-Eight

JANE

Groaning, I stretch and let out a hiss. Damn, I'm still sore. Although, I suppose a few days isn't really long enough to heal from a stab wound that almost kills you. Rubbing at my eyes, I sit up a bit to look around the room and find that it's completely empty. That's a bit surprising. I look down to find that someone removed my IV catheter, and a small bandage now covers that spot.

My stomach growls as I shimmy out from under the blankets. Mhm, food sounds delicious right now. I feel gross, though, since I haven't had a shower. I see they must have wiped me down, but that doesn't erase the grimy feeling.

Slowly, I manage to shift my feet off the bed and onto the floor. I have to wait a moment till my head stops spinning before taking a deep breath and pushing myself off the bed. When I don't immediately fall to the ground, I smile and shuffle my way to my bathroom.

Standing in front of the mirror, I assess the damage. Seems I have bandages over the stab wounds. One covers the wound on my front, and another covers the wound on my back. There's a clear film over the bandages that seems to make it waterproof. Since I am already naked, I hobble over to the shower and adjust the knobs to make the water nice and hot.

Once the steam is billowing, I step inside and moan at the feel of the water on my skin. I stand there, letting the water cascade over my head, face, and body. I don't have the energy to actually wash my body, but the feeling of the water already makes me feel better.

My stomach growls again, and I sigh as I turn off the water. Opening the door of the shower, I look up to grab a towel and let out a scream. The pain in my side turns from a dull irritation to a searing fire.

Holding a hand over my chest, I try to get my heart palpitations to slow. I narrow my gaze at the male in my bathroom and snap, "Holy fucking shit, Jace! You about gave me a heart attack! Must I remind you that I was stabbed by the last person hiding in my bathroom?!"

He winces as he walks over. Handing me a towel, he says, "I'm sorry, Princess. I heard the shower turn on and wanted to make sure you were okay. You seemed fine, but I wanted to stay in case something happened."

Snatching the towel from him, I growl. "Announce yourself next time." I wrap the towel around me and hold my injured side. "Fucking hell," I hiss out.

Jace helps guide me back into my room, and I look up to find three other men racing into my room. I roll my eyes as I gently lower myself onto the bed. Jace jogs into my closet. I smirk. Seems I made him feel bad enough to grab my clothes for me.

Zane looks around the room and asks, "What happened? We heard you scream."

I smirk up at him. "Good to know my scream will have you come running."

He glares at me with an arched brow. I roll my eyes and explain, "Jace was in the bathroom and just stood there like a creeper. I didn't know he was there, so when I opened the shower door—" I shrug. "He scared the shit out of me, and now my side hurts like a bitch."

Jace jogs back into the room, holding my clothes. He hands them to me and says, "I'm sorry, Princess. I should have let you know I was there."

I sigh. "It's fine. Just for future reference, let me know you're in the room."

Alec comes over, grabbing the underwear for me. He kneels on the ground and slips my legs through each hole before grabbing my pants and doing the same. Standing, he holds his hands out to me. "Up you get, Moonbeam."

Howe comes to my other side, grabbing my bra and shirt. Slipping my hands into Alec's, he helps me stand, and Howe reaches out an arm for me to hold onto. Smiling, I hold onto Howe as Alec kneels again to shimmy my clothes up my legs and over my ass.

Alec holds onto my hips as Howe helps me slip into my sports bra and a loose t-shirt. I didn't think I needed help getting dressed, but I wasn't about to refuse since they offered.

Now clean and dressed, I clap my hands. "Food! I need food!"

Alec and Howe grin as they slip a hand through each other's arms. Alec gives me a peck on the cheek as Howe says, "We prepared quite the spread, Starlight."

Jace exits the room first, and I'm ushered after. I notice that Zane waits until we pass before he follows behind. Seems that the protection formation has made its way into my everyday life.

Making conversation, I clear my throat and ask, "So, can I get my face tattoo now?"

Jace glances at me over his shoulder as we enter the kitchen. He arches a brow. "You want your face tattoo?"

I nod as I take a seat at the table. A plate of food is already sitting in front of me. Scooping up some eggs, I shovel them into my mouth and moan as I chew. Fuck, I love food. Before I take another bite, I say, "Yeah, I figure I've earned it."

Zane sits down beside me, frowning as he asks, "Did you think you had to earn your facial tattoo?"

Giving up on being polite, I answer with food in my mouth, "No."

"So what do you mean?" Jace asks.

I shrug. "I've been wanting to get it, but you guys keep saying no. Figured I've earned it now. So, can I get my tattoo now?"

I look up in time to watch Alec and Howe facepalm at the same time. Jace shakes his head while sighing, and Zane rubs at his temples with a frown. I arch a brow. "What? What did I say?"

"We never said you couldn't get it because you had to earn it," Zane says with a growl.

Jace picks up, saying, "We said you couldn't get your tattoo because it takes weeks to heal. We wanted you established as Persephone before you were absent from the meetings for a few weeks."

I tap the fork to my lips. That makes sense, although . . . "I've been gone from the meetings the last few days, so a few more weeks won't matter, will it?" I'm trying to hide my grin because I'm just fucking with them. I don't really care if I get my tattoo right now, but I haven't been able to fuck with Jace the last few days. Plus, the stabbing really put a damper on everyone's mood. We needed some normalcy. What better way than me fucking with them?

Zane glares at me. "You were just stabbed a few days ago. We are not adding to the healing process."

Alec must catch on to what I'm doing because he calls me out, "You little tease. Stop fucking with them."

I smile as I reply, "I should probably just throw a lamp at him."

Confused by my sudden change in subject, all the guys give me confused looks. Howe's the first to ask, "Throw a lamp at him?"

I nod, pointing between Jace and Zane. "Both of them, I think. Just throw a lamp at them."

Alec is still confused. "Why would you throw a lamp at them?"

I snort a laugh and joke, "So they would lighten the fuck up."

It takes a moment for my words to sink in, but when they do, Howe and Alec both howl in laughter. Jace and Zane both send me a glare, but I can see the laughter in their eyes.

I shrug, then continue to eat with a smirk on my face. I don't really care about the facial tattoo, but I love pissing off my two major-alpha men. I also wanted to lighten the mood, considering they have been overly stressed and in protective mode the last few days.

"What's the plan for today?" I ask a little while later as I make my way over to the couch to settle down. I grab one of the fluffy pillows to rest against my painful side.

Howe shrugs as he flops down beside me. Alec nestles down on my other side and replies, "We could chill and watch some movies."

I nod. "That sounds great!"

Jace sits down in front of me between my legs. He pulls one of my feet into his lap and starts massaging. I groan, letting my head fall against the back of the couch. I love foot massages.

"We should call Silas and Jax and let them know Jane is doing okay," Zane says.

I open my eyes enough to see where he's sitting. He took the loveseat beside the couch. Closing my eyes again, I mumble, "We should invite them over for movie night."

Jace squeezes my foot softly, saying, "We can do that."

I enjoy the warmth surrounding me and the soft caress of Jace's hands on my feet. Before I even realize it, I fall into darkness.

I come awake when I hear voices whispering around me. When I feel the fire blazing on my side, I let out a groan. Fuck, I didn't take any meds. As if reading my mind, Jace's warm voice greets me. "I have some meds for you, Princess."

Squinting my eyes open, I notice that the room is darker than when I fell asleep. Jace stands in front of me, holding out two pills and a glass of water. Reaching out for the meds, I smile and say, "Thank you." Popping the meds into my mouth and quickly taking a gulp of water, I groan again as I lean back into the couch.

Looking around, I grin when I see that Silas and Jax are here. "Hey, guys!"

They both look over at me as Jax grins and says, "Sleeping Beauty has finally woken up."

"Not sure how long I'll stay awake, but yeah," I respond with a smirk.

"Don't mind us. Sleep if you need to," Silas says from beside Jax.

"I'll stay awake for as long as I can. It would be rude to fall asleep on you guys right now."

Silas shakes his head. "Don't worry about being rude. If you need rest, then rest."

I smile, looking between the two of them. I didn't realize that I had started to care for them as much as I do. Like two protective brothers I never had and didn't know I wanted or needed. "You guys worry too much."

"Apparently, we don't worry enough, considering you got stabbed and all," Jax says.

I snort out a laugh. "You sound like the guys now."

"With good reason, apparently," Silas grunts out.

I grin as I snuggle down into the couch, surrounded by the warmth of my men. Surrounded by my family.

Chapter Twenty-Nine

JANE

It's been a week since I was stabbed, and my side is healing nicely. I'm still sore, but I'm moving around much better than I was. The guys are still being a bit overprotective, but I'm going along with it for now. I know I went through a traumatic event, not only just for myself but for them as well. I can only imagine what it would be like to see the person you love bleeding out and slowly dying.

I sigh as I make my way down the stairs. Zane is the only one home with me today because the others had to do some stuff for work. I have to admit; I do not miss the meetings.

For the last few days, I've been craving something sweet, but the guys don't keep many sweets in the house. Heading toward the kitchen, I start my search for the ingredients I will need to make chocolate chip cookies. Humming to myself, I grin as I gather everything. Sweet!

I should have an hour or so before Zane will be looking for me after his workout, so I can make the cookies and sit down while they bake. That way, he can't be upset. I only have a few more ingredients to mix in when Zane walks in earlier than I expected. Well . . . damn.

"What are you doing up?" he asks with a growl.

I roll my eyes as I mix in the last few ingredients. Popping a chocolate chip in my mouth, I say, "I'm making cookies."

Coming to stand in front of me, he says, "I can see you're making cookies, but that doesn't answer the question as to why you are up?"

I roll my eyes again. "I wanted something sweet, and there wasn't anything in the house that fit that description. I'm making some cookies to fix my need for something sweet." I hold up the bowl of cookie dough as if to emphasize my point.

"I could have made them!" he argues.

I snort out a laugh. "You have no idea how to make cookies, Zane."

"I would have figured it out. You could have been resting while I was making them. All you had to do was ask," he grumbles.

Feeling a spark of irritation, I snap, "I'm not a delicate flower, Zane. I can make cookies!"

Looking up from my cookie-making, I find him frowning. Then the frown turns to a sneer as he yells, "You should be resting! You almost fucking died, Sunshine!"

Trying to keep my anger under control, I take a deep breath. Puffing out a gust of air, I reply, "I know, Zane, but I feel better. I can't just lie around anymore; I'm going crazy."

Zane runs a frustrated hand through his hair. "Just fucking rest, woman! I don't care if it's making you crazy!"

I stop mixing and point my spatula at him, glaring up at him as I yell back, "I'm fucking Persephone! I'm not a wilting flower, you overbearing asshole!"

His eyes narrow on me as he growls out, "I'm Thanatos! Of course, I'm a fucking asshole and overbearing. I'm overbearing because *my* fucking *Sunshine* will not rest after almost dying!" His chest is heaving from emotion as his eyes pierce mine.

Standing a little taller, I reply, "And I'm your fucking Queen. I say I'm fine, so settle, or else."

He sneers as he spits out, "Or else what, my Queen?"

I smirk as I walk around the counter so I'm in front of him. What he doesn't know is that I have an egg hidden behind my back. I arch a brow as I say, "Or else this." His brows arch, and I swing my arm out from behind me and smash the egg on top of his head.

His eyes widen as the gooey egg runs down his dark-brown hair, making its way into the bun on the top of his head from working out. My eyes widen as well because, holy shit, I actually did it.

"Did you really just smash an egg onto my head, Sunshine?" he asks with a bit of surprise hinting in his tone.

I bite the edge of my lip, unsure how to respond. "Um . . . yes?"

His eyes narrow. "That seems like you're asking me. Did you smash an egg in my hair, Jane?"

OH. Shit. Forgetting my cookies, I duck around him and run toward my room like my life depends on it. Hearing his stomping feet following behind me, I squeal but don't look back. Those women who look back in a horror movie are stupid. Why the fuck would you look back?!

I screech when his arms wrap around my waist and lift me off the ground before I get to my door. His breath whispers across my ear as he promises darkly, "You are going to pay for that, Sunshine."

He moves so he's holding me bridal style so as not to hurt my side. I grin up at him as I taunt, "Is that so? How will I be paying for it?"

Zane stares down at me, and I can see the fire behind his eyes. Suddenly, I'm hot for a completely different reason. "You will be washing the egg out of my hair."

We make our way into my room, rounding the corner and heading to my bathroom. He sets me on the counter as he begins to strip. I bite my lip as he reveals his body in its full naked glory. His nipple piercings are sexy as fuck. I wonder if they are sensitive . . .

He turns toward the shower, wiggling the knobs to turn the hot water on. Turning back around, he arches a brow and asks, "You coming in dressed?"

Shaking my head, I jump down from the counter. I strip quickly, not wanting to waste any time. I haven't had a chance to do anything sexual with Zane yet . . . not for the lack of trying, though. So if this is my chance to have time with him, I am going to take it. Stepping out of my underwear, I look up to find Zane watching me. His eyes seem to darken as they roam over me, but they change the moment he sees the bandage still covering my stab wound.

Not wanting the mood to change, I step into the shower. I turn to him, smiling as I say, "Get your hair wet if you want me to wash it."

He shifts under the stream of water, doing as I say. After his hair is completely soaked, he hands me the shampoo. I smirk and tell him, "You're going to have to kneel. I can't reach the top of your head."

The corner of his lips tilt up as he nods and drops to his knees in front of me. I pour a good amount of shampoo into my hands and start lathering up his hair. I feel his hands come up and rest on my hips and smile as I continue with his hair.

I feel the press of his lips against the bandage on my abdomen. Dropping my eyes, I find him staring intently at the bandage as he brushes it lightly with his finger.

I wash the soap off my hands before pressing my hand against his cheek. He huffs out a sigh as he nuzzles into my hand. Brushing my thumb across his cheek, I say softly, "I'm really okay. I promise."

He looks up at me, and I can see the battle waging in his eyes. The one between his head and heart. Logically, he knows I'm okay, but his heart isn't convinced yet. I shift a bit to lower so that my lips lightly brush his. "Rinse that soap out of your hair, and I'll show you just how okay I am," I whisper.

I smile as I pull away; slipping out of the shower and wrapping a towel around me, I move over to my bed. I hear the water shut off only seconds after I lie down. I watch the bathroom door until Zane walks out with a towel wrapped around his abdomen.

He makes his way over to me slowly, and I watch his every move. Water is still dripping off of him and down his face. He stands in front of me now, gazing down at me with more hunger than I could have ever imagined possible from him.

I smile up at him and pull my towel away from my body. He sucks in a breath; his voice is gravelly when he says, "Move up the bed."

I shimmy up toward the headboard and watch him kneel on the bed. He makes his way up the bed until he's hovering over me. He gives me a once-over before looking me in the eyes. I can see his hesitation in them as he whispers, "We shouldn't. You haven't healed enough."

Pushing his towel off with my feet, I grin when I see his cock standing at full attention. My eyes meet his again, and I state, "I want you, and you obviously want me."

He huffs out a breath. "Of course, I want you, Sunshine."

I lift my hips so my molten-hot center brushes against his cock. He sucks in a breath as I do it again. "Fuck me, Zane. Or I'll find someone else who will."

His eyes flare with anger as he sits up enough to position his cock against my entrance. I know I am wet as fuck for him right now. I want his fire. I want his anger. I want the pain. Without warning, he slams into me as he growls. "You want my cock, Jane?"

I whimper at how full I feel. "Yes."

He hovers over me, positioning his hand beside my neck to hold me still. Pulling out, he slams back in. "You want the pain?" he asks.

"Yes," I mumble as I lift my hands and wrap them around his neck so that I can thread my fingers through his hair.

He growls as he pulls out and slams in again. "You want my anger?"

Drops of water fall onto my face from his wet hair, and my side is on fire right now, but I don't care. I need this. I moan as I answer him, "Yes."

He grunts but picks up the pace of his brutal fucking. I tug him down and smash my lips to his before pulling away enough to nip and bite at his lip piercing. He groans as he pumps into me over and over again. I force my lips to his again, and our tongues tangle as we fight for dominance.

I can feel my orgasm building. Fuck, I need more. Pulling my lips away from his, I huff out, "Faster . . . Harder . . ."

He does as I ask and picks up the pace. I whimper from the pleasure. I need the pain. I want the pain. It makes me feel real. It makes me feel alive. Opening my eyes, I look into Zane's. I can see the battle waging in them. The battle between not wanting to hurt me and giving me what I want.

I release my grip on his hair to cup his face in both hands. Looking deep into his ice-blue eyes, I pant, "I'm here. I'm alive."

He stares into my eyes for a moment, and I see the switch in him as he slams his lips to mine. He pumps a few times before I swallow his roar as he comes. My orgasm is not far behind as I milk the last of his orgasm from him.

We lie there, not moving, just breathing in each other and this moment. He pulls away, and his ice-blue eyes meet mine again as he shifts to run his fingers through my hair. We are still connected, but I don't mind. I think he needs this just as much as I do.

"I love you, Sunshine," he whispers.

I smile as I say, "I love you too, Zane."

He presses his lips softly against mine before pulling away again. "Don't ever do that again, okay? Not even you are allowed to take my sunshine away."

My smile softens. "I'll try."

Chapter Thirty

JANE

It's officially been two weeks since my stabbing, and I've finally convinced the guys to allow me to walk around the compound so long as it's with other Hellhounds. Silas and Jax needed a day off, and the guys couldn't follow me around because they had better things to do. My men had finally caved when I'd pointed out that not only did Silas and Jax vet all of the Hellhounds, but Howe had too. We should be safe now. I hope.

So here I am now, being followed around by a thirty-something . . . maybe forty-something guy. He can't have been here for more than a few weeks because he doesn't seem to remember the protocols. I had asked him what his name was, and he had blurted out, "Chad!"

I facepalmed and asked, "What's your code name?"

"Viper."

Viper? That was the oddest code name for a Hellhound I had ever heard, but who was I to judge? I am enjoying my small bits of freedom while I can. I look behind me to find Chad—ugh, what an unfortunate name—looking shifty AF. He looks at me, and his eyes widen, so I arch a brow and ask, "You good?"

He rubs the back of his head as he smiles awkwardly, "Of course, Miss Persephone."

My eyes narrow for a moment, then I turn back around. Just when I'm about to turn the corner to head back into the cave, there's a sudden pain in my neck. I try to bat at it, but my body slumps to the floor before I can do anything.

"I'm so sorry, Miss Persephone." I hear him say.

I growl as my body loses the battle against whatever drug is dragging my body into the darkness. Two thoughts go through my head before I succumb. One, fucking hell, the guys won't allow me anywhere without them now. Two, never trust a fucking Chad.

When I wake, my brain is cloudy. I groan as I try to shuffle, but something halts my movements. What the hell? I'm tied to a chair. Lifting my head, I look around the dark room until my eyes focus on a male seated in the corner. Fuck. I thought I had finally been able to hide from this man.

"Hello, daughter."

"Father." Son of a bitch! I groan in pain. The stab wound in my abdomen is still healing, and the odd position I'm in right now isn't helping.

"I bet you're wondering why you are here, Sweetheart."

"Please tell me you aren't going to go off on a villainous monologue." Huffing a laugh, I say, "They are so overdone." A chair screeches across the floor, and I look up to find my father has moved, so he's right before me.

"Well, I wouldn't call it a villainous monologue. But I may as well tell you why you are here before your new husband shows up." He shrugs.

Lifting a brow in question, I ask, "Husband? I hope you didn't sell off my virginity, Father. We both know that's long gone."

His laugh echoes in the dark room, startling me. "Sweetheart, we both know virginity doesn't sell like it used to. What man wants a blubbering, bleeding bride when he can have a woman with more experience? Virgins have become a hassle in the black market."

"How did you marry me off legally?"

He grins wickedly. "All I needed was something with your handwriting. There's a man who does an impeccable forgery of your signature. All I had to do was get a marriage certificate and the male who wished to buy you."

He shrugs again. "Completely legal in the eyes of the government. You can't prove that his signature isn't yours. And once the male comes to receive you, you will disappear in the system."

He stands. Walking up to me, he pats my cheek. "I would advise you to do as you're told with this male, daughter. He has a dark fetish for the females he buys." He walks toward the exit, and I struggle against my bindings. Turning to look at me once more with an evil smile, he informs me, "The females often find themselves . . . disappearing." Then he leaves the room, slamming the door closed behind him. Well that doesn't bode well for me.

I struggle a little longer but have to stop. The pain in my abdomen is making me breathless. I face the door and refuse to close my eyes in case my new keeper walks in. After what feels like hours, I feel my eyes getting heavier, but I know I can't fall asleep! I can't ...

When I hear the rattle of the door handle. I startle awake. I watch as the door opens and let out a gasp. No. No! Anyone but him! His sinister smile greets me. "Hello, Pet."

I try to keep the fear at bay. "Doyle." This man was one of my father's best friends. He was one of the males who touched and assaulted me as a child. Fucking hell. He's the one who bought me? The fear inside me is building, but I try to keep my mask of indifference in place. The moment he knows I'm afraid is the minute he wins.

He closes and locks the door behind him. "I'm going to have so much fun with you, Pet. Do you know how long I've waited to have you? The fantasies I have had . . ." He shivers with excitement, and I watch as he adjusts his pants. I can't help but notice that he's turned on.

I can't stop my grimace as memories assault me. Images of him smiling and leering at me as a child. I whisper, "Please don't do this, Doyle."

His breathing speeds up, and his eyes flare with excitement. "Yes, my Little Pet. Beg for me." He stands in front of me and releases some of the bindings holding me to the chair. My hands are still bound, though. He grips my hair tightly, almost ripping it out in the process. I can't stop the squeak of pain that passes through my lips, and I see his nostrils flare. He groans. "Yes, Little Pet. I want to hear your cries. Your screams."

He drags me out of the chair, and I have to move my legs quickly to avoid falling to the ground. I hear water dripping, and I try to look up enough to see where we are headed. Unfortunately, I can't see much due to his hold on my head. The closer we get, I notice that the floor is wet.

I hold in a gasp when I realize that my face is hovering over a large metal basin with water spilling over the edge.

"Did you know that when you hold a person underwater, they will try to hold their breath for as long as possible?" he taunts.

Keeping my voice steady, I answer, "Yes. The instinct to not inhale the water is too strong for a person to fight. They will fight the person holding them under for as long as possible."

He hums in appreciation. "Yes. The instinct to not inhale is so strong that a person will not try to breathe until they are about to pass out."

"Yes."

I can hear the grin in his voice as he says, "Let's see how long you last, Pet." Then, before I can take a deep breath, he shoves my head underwater. At first, I don't fight because I know that's what he wants. But the longer he holds me under, the harder it is to fight the instinct to push against his hold. Finally, I'm about to start fighting when he yanks my head out by my hair. suck in a much-needed breath of air. "Not bad, Pet. But I think I can make you fight." Then he shoves me under again.

I can't stop myself this time. I shove against the basin, trying to free myself. I know this is using up vital oxygen, but I can't stop. My only thought is getting oxygen. I need oxygen. Darkness closes in around me, and I can't fight anymore. I open my mouth and scream out my frustration.

I'm taking in a breath underwater as he pulls my head out. I cough out the water, vomiting in the process.

"Oh, Pet, you lasted longer than any of my other toys. You are going to be so much fun. So much fun to break." Using my hair again, he drags me across the floor and into a cell in the corner. I didn't even notice it was there. He tosses me inside so quickly that I can't stop my head from slamming against the floor. The darkness drags me into its cold embrace once more.

I'm not sure how long I've been here. It's been days. Or maybe weeks. I'm not entirely sure. Time is irrelevant when you are tortured to the point you pass out. Also, fuck Hollywood. They gave me the wrong impression of torture for women. Or maybe I just watched the wrong movies to give me a better idea of what I was dealing with. In the movies I watched, the women walked away with only a few scratches, and their makeup still looked immaculate.

I look like a wet dog that has been abandoned for years. Well, from what I could glimpse in the water before my head was shoved under. My hair was tangled to the point I had to tie it up with a piece of fabric I ripped off my shirt. Although who am I trying to impress? A wave of sadness washes over me. I miss my men so much it hurts. I'm a sad excuse of a Persephone right now, but I know my men will come for me.

Chapter Thirty-One

JANE

Doyle walks into the room like he always does. With a smile and a hard-on. He surprisingly hasn't raped me yet. Which, don't get me wrong, I'm happy about, but also I wish he would just get it over with. The waiting for it to happen is killing me. Although, he does rub one out after each session. Doesn't take him much. While I'm lying on the floor, gasping for air with a few more bruises to add to my ever-growing collection, he whips out his disgusting cock and pumps like three times. I try to hold back my gag because he always comes all over me; this time will be no different.

My clothes are soaked in dirt and come. God, I need to get this shit off me. Doyle leans down in front of me with a grin and taunts, "How are we today, Pet? You ready for some fun?"

I don't answer. It seems to piss him off when I don't answer, and considering my body won't listen to my brain, it's all I have.

His grin dims a bit as he growls. "Fine, Pet." Gripping my hair tightly, he drags me over to my usual torture spot.

Fuck, I'm so tired. I'm starting to wish he would just let me die. Which is a horrid thought considering I want to be found, but I'm finding it hard to care anymore. He's holding my head above the water basin when suddenly I hear a popping sound. My foggy mind tries to remember what that sound is, but to be honest, I'm way too exhausted to figure it out. Doyle's fingers loosen his hold on my hair; then I hear a loud thump. Hum . . . weird. Still staring down at the water, I realize it's turning red. Why's the water turning red? Wasn't the water clear earlier . . . or was it dirty? I can't remember. Wait . . . where did Doyle go?

It takes a lot of work, but eventually, I force my aching body to turn so I can figure out where my torturer went. My eyes meet his toes, then his legs. Continuing upward, I realize that he's lying on the floor. That's not normal. Did he fall asleep while torturing me? That would be an odd thing to do, right? My eyes finally reach his face, but he doesn't have much of a face now. Just chunks of flesh and blood. Lots of blood. That's a disturbing amount of blood. I should probably be freaking out, right? Somehow, I don't have it in me to care.

"Jane?"

I stiffen when I hear my name. I haven't heard that voice in what feels like forever. That deep and playful voice. "Jax?" I whisper. My voice is scratchy from screaming and lack of use. I'm too afraid to look. Too scared that this is only a dream, and when I turn around, he'll have disappeared.

"Hey, Sweets," he chokes out.

My eyes jerk up to find Jax in the doorway with a gun resting at his side. His hazel eyes are locked on mine. Suddenly, Silas is behind him, his eyes wild as he takes in the room. His eyes lock on mine, and he calls out, "Jane!"

My knees give out, and I collapse to the floor. They came. "You came." My voice is quiet, but I know they heard me.

They rush over to me, hands outstretched to touch me but hesitant. Their worried eyes roam over my body, and I can only imagine what they see. Silas grunts as he says, "Of course we came, Jane. We've been looking for you for two weeks!"

"Where are the guys?" Not that I'm not thankful for Jax and Silas, I just wanted to know where my guys were.

"They are currently dealing with your father," Jax growls out.

I nod. That makes sense. Not that I wouldn't be happy if they were the ones to save me, but I'm glad they aren't here to see what I look like right now. "I need a shower, please." I try to raise my voice, but it only comes out as a hoarse whisper.

The brothers look at each other before Jax turns to me and nods. "We seem to be in the basement of this guy's house, but he has a bathroom upstairs."

I grit my teeth as I try to force myself to get up. Jax seems to see my struggle, so he softly wraps his arms around me. Putting one arm under my shoulders and the other under my knees, he lifts me into the air, and I try not to grimace in pain. My whole body fucking hurts.

"I'm sorry," he whispers.

"It's okay."

He slowly carries me out of the room I've been held in and up some stairs. Silas leads the way, opening the door to what I assume is the upstairs. I don't even realize that I've closed my eyes until Jax whispers, "You okay, Jane?"

I open my eyes to find that we are in a large bathroom. I look around to find a shower. Nodding, I whisper back, "Yes. Just tired."

He nods as he sets me down on the bathroom counter. I guess he doesn't trust that I can stand on my own. He isn't wrong, though. He walks to the shower and opens the sliding glass door to start the water. It takes only a few seconds before there's steam billowing into the room. Silas comes into the room with some clothes for me, and I raise a brow in question.

He shrugs. "I figured you probably didn't want to wear those clothes anymore. I found another bedroom with some women's clothes in it. Figured it was better than wearing that rapist's clothes."

He has a point. Setting the clothes down on the counter beside me, he turns to walk back out of the room. "DON'T LEAVE," I cry. My throat hurts, but I don't care.

He turns to look at me with wide eyes. "I was only going to wait outside the room."

I shake my head and beg, "Please, don't leave." As I look toward the shower, I feel my panic growing. Jax is still next to the shower, and my eyes meet his. "I can't get in there. The water . . . I . . . can't."

His eyes narrow for a moment before widening. His voice comes out hoarse as he asks, "He forced your head underwater? That was what was in the basin?"

I nod. "It's closed in. I'll feel trapped. I . . . I don't know if I can handle my head being under the spray." I feel like I'm about to have a panic attack as my heart starts to race, and I can't catch my breath.

A loud growl sounds beside me, and I turn my head to watch as Silas stomps over to the shower. Without a thought, he rips the glass doors off with a grunt. Wow. Fucking hell, that's impressive. He looks at Jax in silent question. Jax bites his lip and nods. He leaves the room briefly before coming back in, in what I assume are clothes from Doyle's closet.

Walking over, he lifts me off the counter and lets my toes settle on the ground right outside the shower. He looks back over to Silas, and I follow his gaze to find Silas bringing over a towel. Handing the towel to Jax, he turns so he's no longer facing me. I look back to Jax, raising a brow in question. I'm too exhausted to do anything else.

He gives me a sad smile and gently explains, "Here's the plan, Sweets. I'm going to hold up this towel, and you're going to strip. Once you're done, wrap the towel around you. I'll get in and help with your hair and face. I'll get out after that, and you can wash the rest of your body."

My eyes widen. "You'll get soaked!"

His smile turns more genuine as he says, "That's why I changed into the fucker's clothes." He raises the towel up so he can't see me. I quickly strip out of the disgusting clothes and grab the towel from his hands. I notice his eyes closed, and I can't help but smile. Wrapping the towel around me quickly, I say. "I'm covered."

He squints one eye open to verify before opening both and nodding. He helps steady me as we walk into the shower. Grabbing the shower head, he slowly runs it over my hair. My eyes close, and my breath quickens each time he gets close to my face, but he always makes sure the spray never hits. The spray pauses in my hair; then gentle fingers wipe at my face softly. I open my eyes slowly to see Jax's pensive expression, his eyes full of concentration.

He must feel my eyes on him because his eyes meet mine briefly before going back to my face. "What?" he asks.

I can't stop the small smile as I say, "You're acting like an older brother."

He snorts and replies, "I am an older brother."

I close my eyes and whisper, "But you're not *my* older brother."

His hands pause for a moment on my face. "We're family. So . . . that makes me your older brother."

I bite my lip and nod. I can't let my emotions out yet; I need to stay strong for a little while longer. He continues to clean off my face before starting on my hair. He had to wash it three times before he said it was clean. Pressing his lips to my forehead, he pulls away. I open my eyes to watch him step out and immediately sit on the ground beside Silas, facing away from me.

"Don't you want to change out of your wet clothes?"

He shakes his head. "I'll change once you're done."

Looking over at Silas, I see he has two towels in his lap. He hands one to Jax, who wraps it around himself. I take a deep breath, then let the wet towel hit the floor. It makes a splat, and I push it out of the way. Grabbing the soap, I lather myself up. I scrub and scrub until my skin is bright pink, but no matter how hard I scrub, I can't get the feel of Doyle off of me.

Eventually, I let the dirty suds swirl around my feet before shutting off the water.

I turn to find that Silas already has the towel held out for me to grab. I take it and wrap it around myself tightly. Jax and Silas stand, and I reach out to grasp Jax's arm. He turns just enough to ensure I'm covered before wrapping an arm around me to help me walk to the bathroom counter. He waits until I have my balance before turning back around.

I lean against the counter to slide my underwear and pants on first. There isn't a bra, so I just slip the large shirt over my aching body. "I'm dressed."

The brothers turn to face me. I look between the two of them before stopping on Silas. I've only asked the question once before, and I know he isn't an affectionate guy, but . . . I really need this. "Hey, Silas. Can I ask a favor?"

He nods. "Of course."

My fingers tangle in my shirt before I ask in a whisper, "Can I have a hug?" Before I can even look up to see his reaction, he's in front of me, wrapping me in his arms. Fuck. I needed this. My arms wrap around him, and I grip his shirt lightly. His hold isn't tight, just enough to make me feel safe. "Thank you," I whisper brokenly.

"For what?"

"For saving me."

He makes a grunting sound before holding me tighter. "You are family. I'll always come for you."

And with those words, the floodgates open. Every ounce of fear, pain, and loneliness I've kept inside pours out. I sob into his chest as my fingers dig into his back. I just want to feel that he's real, that this isn't a dream.

I hear his whispered words as he holds me tight. "We've got you. You're safe now."

Chapter Thirty-Two

JANE

I'm in the passenger seat as Silas drives us back to the house, and to be honest, I'm a little nervous. Fuck, I look like shit. I tug at my shirt again. Silas places one hand over mine as he drives with the other. "Stop fidgeting."

"I'm nervous," I whisper.

"Why are you nervous? It's just the guys," Jax asks from the back of the car.

"I look like shit!" I cry.

Jax snorts a laugh and says, "You look like a woman who has survived two shitty weeks. They don't care what you look like, Sweets. They'll just be so happy that you're home."

Silas gives my hand one last squeeze before he switches hands to roll down the window. He puts in the gate code, then rolls the window up. The iron gates open, and we make our way down the long drive. Before we make it to the house, though, Silas stops the car. I'm confused until I see four men racing down the drive toward us. I unbuckle my seatbelt, but before I can turn to open the door, it's ripped open.

I'm suddenly lifted into someone's arms. I wince slightly because, holy shit, my body hurts. Whoever is holding me pulls back, and I can see that it's Alec. His eyes are wide, and tears are streaming down his face. "I'm sorry! Did I hurt you?"

I shake my head. "No. I'm okay, just sore."

He gives me one last look over before I'm lifted into the air again. I look behind me to see Howe giving me a bear hug. "I fucking missed you, Starlight."

I attempt a grin as I say, "I missed you too." He sets me down softly, and I turn to find Jace and Zane watching me. I can tell they are holding back. My two tough men. Slowly, I make my way over to Zane first, wrapping my arms around him. He stiffens for a moment before wrapping his arms around me and returning the hug.

His voice is strained as he says, "Fuck, Sunshine."

I pull away just enough to croak, "Take me home." Suddenly, I'm in Jace's arms, and he marches to the house. His body shakes with each step, and I know he's trying to stay strong because Silas and Jax are following behind in the car. He doesn't want to show weakness.

The door to the house is wide open, so we walk right on through and up to the bedrooms. I notice that we don't go to mine. Instead, he takes me to a different bedroom that doesn't belong to any of them. He walks through the door and takes me to the large bed in the center of the room. The bed is big enough that all five of us will fit.

He lays me on my back, then snuggles as close as he can get to my side. He shoves his face into my neck and takes a deep breath. He doesn't speak just keeps breathing. Zane follows behind and settles on my other side, snuggling in just as close.

Howe and Alec settle by my legs, oddly snuggling with my feet. But, whatever. No judgment. I am happy to have all of them touching me.

I feel Jace's breath hitch against my neck, and I know he's trying to hold everything in. When I look over to Zane, I find him with his eyes squeezed shut while he bites his lip. My poor men. What the hell is wrong with society that men aren't allowed to show emotion? What's wrong with men crying when they need to cry? I also know these two men blame themselves for not protecting me.

My voice is still scratchy, but I manage to say, "I don't blame you. And if you really need forgiveness for something that isn't your fault, then . . . I forgive you." I lift my arms enough so that I can caress their cheeks. It's awkward, but I make it work. "Let it out. Keeping it all bottled up will only make it hurt more."

I feel them both shift their faces closer to my neck, so I can't turn my face to see theirs. That's fine. They can hide if they need to. They're both quiet, but I can hear the change in their breaths. Unsteady and clipped. Harsh and wet.

Being surrounded by their warmth, keeping my eyes open is hard. Between one breath and the next, I fall into oblivion.

I moan as my brain starts to wake. Fuck, my body hurts. Also, I'm starving! The smell of the woods and fire surrounds me. Mhm. Jace and Zane. I smile as I open my eyes and see that both are snuggled up as close as they can get to me. Shifting my gaze down to my feet, I see Howe and Alec are already awake. They whisper back and forth as they sit on the edge of the bed. Each of them has a hand resting on my feet, which makes my smile grow.

I clear my throat just loud enough for them to hear me but not loud enough to wake the two sleeping males beside me. Howe's and Alec's gazes shift to me quickly, and they each give me a sad smile.

I whisper, "Do I look that bad?"

They shake their heads, then Alec quietly speaks, "You always look beautiful. Although, I have to say it's a good thing you didn't get your face tattoo a few weeks ago. I think it may have been ruined if you had."

I grimace. Yeah . . . that's what I had been thinking too. I don't know how it would have held up after being waterboarded and beaten. My stomach lets out a loud growl, and I feel my face heat. "I think I'm a bit hungry. You guys mind helping me out of this pile of limbs?"

Howe looks at Alec before saying, "We can make you something. I think these two will freak out if they wake up and you're not here."

Alec nods in agreement. "They have been a bit wild since you went missing. They haven't slept much either."

"What about you two? How are you?" I ask.

Howe shrugs and replies, "We are usually the ones who try to keep their hopes up. We knew we would find you, but these two go feral when it comes to you."

Alec gives my foot a squeeze before standing. "We knew we would find you, but we had to make sure Jace and Zane believed that too. I'll go make you something quick. Something small and light, so it doesn't upset your stomach."

I smile softly up at Alec. "Thank you." He nods, then makes his way out of the room.

Howe gives my foot one last squeeze before he stands and says, "I'll get a bath going for you. I'll make sure there's some stuff in there to help with the soreness."

I nod. "I would love a bath." As long as I keep my head out of the water, I think I'll be fine. I'm snuggled between my two males, so I take a moment to enjoy the feelings of warmth and safety they provide. I feel a hand touch my foot and open my eyes, not realizing I had closed them.

Alec is standing there with a tray and a smile. "I got you toast and fruit. I figured that would be light enough on your stomach. I also got you a small glass of chocolate milk because, as much as I know you would rather have coffee, that may be too harsh right now."

I nod, looking at the males I am currently squashed between. Humming, I try to shimmy myself up the bed to lay against the headboard. Jace and

Zane both mumble but snuggle into my lap once I'm in a seated position. I smirk, looking up at Alec. "I don't think I'll be able to hold the tray."

Alec laughs softly as he makes his way to the side of the bed. He sets the tray down on the side table, then holds out a piece of toast. Smiling at him, I take a few small, tentative bites. Howe returns, smirking when he sees my new position.

"I see they didn't wake up when you moved." He points to Jace and Zane.

I finish chewing my bite of toast before saying, "They must be exhausted. They didn't wake up when I moved."

Howe hums. "They didn't sleep much while you were gone. I'm sure they are making up for days of missed sleep right now."

Alec nods as he says, "Once they wake up, we will show you your surprise."

I grin. "Surprise?"

Howe snorts out a laugh. "Yes, a surprise, but you can't have it until those two wake up."

Looking down at the two sleeping forms in my lap, I debate if I should wake them up to get my surprise but think better of it. I can wait. They haven't had much sleep, so I should let them catch up on rest. I huff out a sigh. "Alright, I suppose I can wait."

Howe and Alec both grin at me. I look around the room and ask, "What should we do while we wait?"

Howe moves over to the side table and opens it, pulling out a remote. I smirk when he turns on the TV, making sure the volume is low. He lays across the bottom of the bed and turns on a movie. I grin when I see that it's Deadpool. That movie will always be a classic go-to no matter what era it is.

Chapter Thirty-Three

JACE

I watch her as she dresses. We have two surprises for her, but the first doesn't involve her getting dressed up as Persephone. I sigh, leaning up against the doorway of the bathroom. I made sure she knew I was here this time before I even entered her bedroom. I'm brought out of my thoughts when I hear my name called. "What?"

She smiles at me in the reflection of the mirror. "Why are you staring at me like that?"

I arch a brow as I ask, "Like what?"

She shrugs and slips her shirt over her bruised skin. I can feel my temper rise again as I remember why she even has those injuries. She was finally healing from the stab wound and then got abducted. Abducted on our watch. I flinch when I feel a hand against my cheek.

She pulls away with worry etched on her face. "Are you alright, Jace?"

I sigh and tell her, "I'm fine, Princess. You didn't answer my question, though."

She smirks as she bounces on her tiptoes and presses a soft kiss to my lips before pulling away. "You were looking at me as if it were the last time you would see me."

I gather her in my arms, holding her close. I hadn't realized I was letting my emotions show so much. "Just making sure I don't take my eyes off you now. Seems like when I do, you vanish."

She gives me a squeeze before pushing away. She slips her hands into mine and looks me in the eyes. "I don't mind you watching me. Means I get more time with you," she says with a smirk.

I snort a laugh and pull her out of the bathroom and the bedroom. We make our way down the stairs. We are headed to the cave to show her the first surprise.

"Are you ready for your first surprise?" Howe asks from the bottom of the stairs.

"I would be more ready if you guys would tell me what to expect," she says with a laugh.

Alec pops his head around the corner, yelling, "You're lucky we even have this surprise. Jace almost ruined it."

Jane looks up at me with a raised brow, and I shrug. I'm not sorry. We caught that betraying viper. It wasn't my fault the man didn't hold up well to torture. I had to get the information about who his employer was somehow. The fucker broke within the first few minutes, and after that, I just wanted blood. Howe had needed to hold me back, and Alec had to hold Zane. I hadn't seen my brother that bloodthirsty in years.

I grin at Jane as she continues to stare at me. "Your surprise may be a little broken, but Howe made sure I didn't break it completely."

Her eyes widen, then she looks at the others. "Well, now I'm curious."

Jane

Walking down the cave compound's corridors, I grin as my guys surround me in a protective bubble. We are heading down to the lower levels of the cave, which makes me curious as to what my surprise could be, considering I've never been in this area before.

My grin widens when I see Jax and Silas at the end of the halfway. It makes a T, but I'm too excited about seeing Jax and Silas. I squeal as I run out of my protective bubble toward Jax first.

Jax's head lifts at the noise, and he grins. "Hey, Sweets!" He opens his arms wide, and I slam into him.

Hugging him tight, I look up at him with a grin. "I didn't know you guys would be coming along too. Do you know what my surprise is?"

He snickers and gives me one last squeeze before releasing me. Nodding, he says, "Of course, I know what it is. I helped with it."

I roll my eyes as I turn to see Silas. The corner of his lips tilt upward as he says, "Hello, Seph." I grin as I make my way over to him. He opens his arms wide enough for a hug if I want one. My grin widens even more when he says, "If you must."

"I must." I laugh and wrap my arms around him. He gives me a soft embrace. Fuck, I love his hugs. I don't know why his are my favorite, but they are. Maybe because he doesn't give hugs to just anyone, so they are special.

He pulls away to look down at me. I watch as his hazel eyes take me in before he huffs out a breath and asks, "How are you doing, Seph?"

"I'm doing much better. Thank you for asking, Alpha."

He gives me a nod as he steps away and points down the hallway behind him. "The surprise is ready for the Queen's viewing."

Well, now I'm extremely excited about my surprise! I look between all my guys before smirking and racing down the hallway. I rip open the door, looking around for my surprise. Honestly, it wasn't the surprise I was expecting, but it's no less surprising. Standing on his tiptoes with his hands wrapped in ropes above his head and hanging from the ceiling is the man who handed me over to my father.

Chad stirs when the door slams against the wall. He slowly raises his head to see who is entering the room. "Please . . . I've told you everything I know," he begs, his voice scratchy. When he sees that it's me, his eyes widen, or should I say eye. His face is covered in blood and bruises. One eye is completely swollen shut, and the other streams with tears as he looks at me.

"Persephone! Please free me! I'm so sorry. I'm sorry! I didn't have a choice," he whimpers as he tries to move in his binds.

I arch a brow as I walk to stand closer to him. "You're sorry that you handed me over to my worst nightmare, or are you sorry you got caught?"

He cries harder as he says, "I'm sorry I handed you over! I didn't have a choice!"

I sneer at this man. Fucking pathetic. I feel like I should be more disgusted by my next actions, but I am tired of people betraying me. I've turned my cheek too many times. It's time to fight back. I hear a huff behind me, and I look over my shoulder to see Zane shaking his head.

Zane sneers. "Have some fucking pride, and grow some fucking balls. Fucking weak-ass motherfucker."

I snort out a laugh. I can't stop from saying, "Balls are weak and sensitive. If you want to be tough, grow a vagina. Those things can take a pounding." I remember hearing that saying somewhere. I think the lady who said it was famous. I think her name was Betty White.

Howe howls in laughter. "So true."

Zane has a small smirk as he says, "Very well. Grow a fucking vagina."

I turn back to Chad, rolling my eyes as he continues to cry. Holding up a hand, I say, "Knife."

There's a shuffle behind me, and a knife is placed in my hand. I grin darkly at the male in front of me as I tap the knife on the fingertips of my other hand. "Let's address 'you had no choice,' shall we?"

He shakes his head wildly. "I didn't have a choice! The man who came to me told me he would kill me if I didn't do it!"

I tap the knife softly against my lips as I circle my prey. Humming, I say, "I see. So you thought you could kidnap me and hand me over without anyone knowing?"

He whines as I slide the knife across his bare skin, making sure not to draw blood but reveling in his weakness. He doesn't answer my question, and I'm about to ask it again before I'm interrupted by a growling voice.

"Answer her fucking questions," Jace demands.

I give him a smirk over my shoulder before turning back to Chad. Ugh, fucking Chad. I arch a brow, tapping the knife against my hand.

He sucks in a breath and answers, "Yes."

I nod. "Such a good little snake. Seems my hounds found you, though." I tap the edge of the knife on his chin. "So the question now is, what should we do with the traitor snake?"

He absolutely loses it. He turns into a blubbering mess with tears seeping from his swollen eye as snot runs down his face. I huff out a sigh and roll my eyes. Fucking hell, this man is weak. I fucking held up to more torture than he has.

Turning, I face my guys, as well as Silas and Jax. "Have the other Hellhounds been briefed on what happens to traitors?"

Silas, in full Alpha mode, nods. "They have, Persephone."

I nod with a dark smile. "Good." Spinning back around, I stab the knife into Chad's thigh. Leaving the knife in his leg, I clap my hands together as he screams. Alright, I'm done with him. He didn't make this fun at all. I turn back around, smirking at Silas and Jax.

I walk up to them just close enough to pat them each on the cheek. Their eyes widen at my actions before I say, "Have fun, hounds. Make sure our snake here can't slither his way back."

Silas and Jax give each other a quick look before looking down at me with a smile. Silas is already moving over to Chad when Jax nods and says, "As you wish, Persephone."

I look to my boys next. "I believe you have another surprise for me?"

Howe prowls over to me and smashes his lips to mine, then pulls away with a groan. "That was hot as fuck."

I smirk up at him and hear Alec snickering behind him. "We'd better take our Queen to see her next surprise before Howe gets any other ideas."

Howe picks me up and throws me over his shoulder as I squeal with laughter. He lands a smack on my ass as he makes his way out of the dungeon. "Who said we can't have a little fun before we give her the next surprise? She has to get changed for it anyway."

I lift my head to see the others following behind. Giving them a smirk, I say, "I wouldn't mind a little fun."

Jace and Zane both snicker as they shake their heads. Alec laughs and teases, "I know you would love to have fun, but I'm sure you will want to see your next surprise more."

Arching a brow, I ask, "Then what's my next surprise?"

Jace huffs. "I suppose we need to tell her, or she will take Howe up on his offer."

Zane's smile turns dark as he says, "We have your father."

My eyes widen at his words. They have my father? My pulse quickens in excitement. I smack Howe's ass and yell, "Well, let's go!" I am finally going to be able to get my revenge against the man who has haunted me.

Chapter Thirty-Four

JANE

I'm sitting on the counter of my bathroom in only my bra and underwear as Howe stands in front of me with a paintbrush in hand. Since Jax is downstairs with Chad, that means he can't do my makeup, so Howe volunteered to do it for me. I'm pretty sure he just wants to spend more time with me.

I'm trying not to smirk as I watch his face. The tip of his tongue is peeking out in concentration as he makes small strokes with the UV paint. I swing my legs a bit to try and keep my face as still as possible. He hasn't put his sclera contacts in yet, so I can see his beautiful hazel eyes. I never realized how light they were. The light-brown color has specks of green.

He must feel my stare because he looks into my eyes, then back up to where he's painting the floral designs on my face. "What?" he asks.

I'm careful not to move my face too much as I say, "Nothing."

He arches a brow. "You've been staring at me the whole time we've been here."

I snort. "Where else am I supposed to look? Plus, you've got a pretty face, might as well enjoy the view."

It's his turn to snort as he says, "Pretty face, huh?"

"Oh, don't act like you don't know you're handsome."

He smiles as he moves to the other side of my face to paint the skull design. "I didn't say I wasn't. It's what most people notice."

I am stunned silent for a moment. Do people only notice that Howe is handsome and focus on his body more than anything else? "You know I love you for more than your body, right?"

He pauses the brush on my face as his eyes widen in surprise. His hazel eyes meet mine again as I continue, "I know you're handsome, Howe, but I think you're extremely smart too. I mean, you have several degrees that you didn't even pay for because you hacked the University systems." I reach up with a hand to press it against his cheek, and his eyes close at the contact. "You are fucking brilliant, Howe. The smartest person I know."

His eyes open, and they swirl with emotion. "Thank you, Starlight."

"Of course," I reply, dropping my hand back down to the counter. I smile as I ask impatiently, "Am I done?"

He arches a brow in confusion until I point to my face. Chuckling, he paints a few more lines before taking a step back. He tilts his head to the side before nodding. "I think it will do. I'm not as good at it as Jax, but it should be fine."

I hop off the counter and turn to see the design. My jaw drops. Holy shit. Howe was seriously downgrading his skill. The paint looks amazing. With my pink UV contacts in and the designs on my face . . . I look amazing. "It's beautiful, Howe."

His cheeks brighten a bit as he shrugs nonchalantly. "Like I said, not as good as Jax."

I turn and shake his shoulder playfully. "It's beautiful. Now go get ready. I'll meet you outside."

He looks around the room before saying, "It's okay. I can wait until you're done."

I understand his hesitation, so I make my way over to him and press my lips gently against his. I pull away just enough to whisper my next words, "I'll be okay. I'll leave the doors open. I'm sure one of the guys is done getting ready. If it would make you feel better, have one of them come in here with me while I finish getting ready."

He presses his lips softly against mine again before backing away with a huff. He nods and says, "I'll get one of the guys to come in here. Leave the doors open, alright?"

I nod as I make my way over to the closet. "It will only take a few minutes for me to get ready. Go get one of the guys. I'll stay alert, I promise."

He gives me one last look before jogging out of the room. I'm just coming out when there's a knock on my bathroom door. I look up to find Alec standing there with a smile.

I grin. "Wow, that was fast."

Alec laughs as he leans against the door jam. "I've never seen Howe run so fast. I thought something was wrong until he said he needed to get dressed and didn't want you to be alone. I was already heading this way, so it didn't take me too long."

Nodding, I slip into the black dress with a slit up to the hip. It has sheer fabric with flowers scattered across it. I must admit; I love the bodice because it has sheer fabric across the abdomen with the boning of the corset black. I turn and look over my shoulder once I'm at the counter. "Can you cinch me up?"

Alec nods and makes his way over to me. His fingers brush lightly against my skin as he laces up the back of my dress. I try to ignore his soft touches as I reach for the newest crown Jace bought to add to my collection. I knew it had to be him because it has a very Hades and Persephone feel. It has golden metal flowers along with dark red rubies. On the front are two vipers holding a deep-red ruby as if protecting it.

I secure the crown into my newly-dyed pastel prism hair looking at myself in the mirror with a smirk. I look fucking badass, if I do say so myself. Alec finishes doing up the laces and turns to grab my heels. He kneels on the ground and holds the first one out to me. I smile down at him as I slip my foot into the black heel with vipers that wrap around my ankles.

He looks up at me with a dark smile and asks, "Are you ready, My Queen?"

My smile matches his as I say, "Let's go have some fun with Daddy dearest."

My heels click as we make our way back down to the dungeons. My heart is beating so fast that I feel like it may beat right out of my chest. The click of my heels echoes around us, and I try to slow my heart to match the sound of my footsteps.

I jerk to a stop right before we get to the door that leads to my father. This . . . this is really happening. A hand settles lightly against the base of my back, and I turn to find Jace looking down at me. "Are you okay, Princess?" he asks, sounding worried.

I nod, looking back at the door. I feel another figure come up beside me. Howe clears his voice, and I turn to find him awkwardly rubbing the back of his neck with a slight blush on his cheeks. He huffs a breath and says, "We sorta got you something."

He pulls out two knives from behind his back, and I arch my brow in question. Where the fuck was he hiding those? I gasp when I look down to find that they aren't ordinary knives but daggers. They each have a curved blade with a delicate handle. The handles are thick but have a thinner knuckle guard. Each one is decorated with small flowers. The first thing that comes to mind is delicate but deadly. They are perfect.

I reach out slowly, taking them from Howe. I shift the daggers to get a better grip and smile at Howe. "Thank you," I say quietly.

He shrugs. "We figured you needed a weapon that's all your own. We also thought the first blood should be your father's."

I can't stop smiling as I nod and turn back to the door. Then, taking a deep breath, I say, "I'm ready." I jump slightly when Jax and Silas step out of the darkness. My eyes widen when I see that they are covered in blood. Although the first thought that comes to mind isn't to ask about the blood, instead, I ask, "Are you guys done with Chad already?"

Jax snorts a laugh. "We decided to end it so we could be here with you when you face your biggest demon."

Silas grumbles, "Like we would let you face your father without us."

The swell of love I feel for these two men fills my chest, and there's a burn behind my eyes as I whisper, "Thank you."

Jax shrugs as he says, "We're family."

I grin as Silas swings open the door to the room my father has been held for the last few days. I stand tall as I enter the room with my real family trailing behind. My eyes widen as I take in the man in front of me. He's tied to a chair in the center of the room but isn't as bloody as I expected. He has a few bruises on his face, but otherwise, he's fine.

I look over my shoulder, arching a brow in question.

Jace shrugs. "There are other ways to torture a man. So I figured his blood was yours to take."

I'm about to ask how the hell he tortured my father when the dim lighting in the room switches to UV lights. My boys' UV tattoos glow bright in the room. I look at Jax and Silas to find their eyes glowing brightly; otherwise, they are dark figures in the room. Fucking . . . creepy.

Turning around, I find that my father has awakened, and his eyes are huge as he looks around the room. Then he screams, causing me to jump at the sound. Fucking hell! I never thought I would hear my father scream, let alone see true panic in his eyes.

Jace comes up to stand beside me with a chuckle as he explains, "If you give a human small doses of hallucinogens, they often see things that aren't there. Then add horrifying men with skulls for faces, and you make a man break in seconds."

I look back at my father and watch as a large wet spot grows in the crotch of his pants. I can't stop myself from giggling. He's panting hard as his eyes look wildly around the room. Finally, his eyes land on me, and he screams, "Get me out of here! Lady, get me out of this room of demons!"

I arch a brow as I make my way over to him. "What makes you think I will help you?"

His eyes widen at the sound of my voice. "Jane?"

I smirk as I stand in front of him. Jax comes up beside me and stabs my father in the neck with a needle. He pushes down the plunger, then throws it on the ground. My father screams in pain as I watch his pupils dilate. Jax snickers beside me and says, "Give it a moment. He'll see you for what you are soon."

Something clicks in my father's eyes as I watch the drug take effect. His mouth opens as if to say something, but I don't give him a chance as I slice my new dagger across his bare thigh. He screams, but I don't pay it any mind as I watch the blood swell from my cut. Hum . . . seems he bleeds red like everyone else.

He pants as he asks, "Why are you doing this, Jane? Do these demons have you under their control?"

I can't help but laugh as I slice across his other thigh. He screams again as I ask, "Did you not realize these demons are mine?"

Tears stream down his face as he huffs out, "Yours?"

I grin darkly as I gesture to the males behind me. "I am their Queen. I am Persephone. My demons and hounds to control."

His eyes widen at my words, and he starts to beg, "Please, don't do this, Jane. I'm your father."

I let out a screech as I slice my dagger across his upper arm. "You were never my father! A father protects! A father loves! You used me! You tried to sell me!" With my next words, I slice across his chest, "You allowed one of your FRIENDS to rape me!"

I'm panting hard as I watch my father cry from the pain. Snot is streaming from his nostrils, and drool is rolling down his chin.

"Stop," he begs as his breathing turns raspy. "Please."

I growl and slam my dagger into his chest. Warm blood sprays across my face as he chokes on his blood. "You never stopped when I asked." His dark eyes meet mine, still pleading for his life. "You never stopped when I said please." I slash across his throat with my other dagger and watch as blood seeps from his neck and mouth.

His eyes widen as he continues to choke on his blood, but I do nothing. I just watch as the life slowly leaves his eyes. My vision blurs momentarily, and I don't realize I'm crying until fingers touch my cheek. I turn to find Jace staring down at me.

"It's okay, Princess. I've got you."

I turn quickly before dropping the dagger and wrapping my arms around him tightly. I feel the others move closer as well. Finally, I hear the gruff voice of Silas as he snarls, "May your soul be devoured in the Underworld. May you never find rest for what you have done."

In that moment, I knew Silas and Jax thought of me as family. My arms tighten around Jace, mostly to stifle my sobs because I have so many emotions running through me. Sadness about losing the father I wish I had. Relief over killing the man who has plagued my nightmares for years. Happiness because I finally have the family I always wished for.

Chapter Thirty-Five

JANE

It's been two weeks since I killed my father. It's like a weight has been lifted off my chest. That's one less person wanting me dead.

A knock on my bedroom door at the mansion makes me jump. We've been hanging out here more often than not due to the threat of the other gang. I peer up from my position on the bed and look toward the door to see Jace leaning against the door frame. I arch a brow as I ask, "What's up?"

The corner of his lip tilts up in a smirk. "The guys and I have been talking, and we think you've healed enough to get your next tattoo."

Jumping up and off the bed in excitement, I squeal. "Are you serious?"

His smirk grows into a full-blown smile as he replies, "We will be leaving in a few for your appointment. So you should probably change out of your pajamas."

I look down at myself. I mean, my pajamas aren't too bad, are they? They're merch from a series written by one of my favorite authors, Britt Andrews. She has this Emerald Lakes series, and the characters talk about penis snails. Made me laugh for hours, and I couldn't pass up buying the pants with penis snails all over them. I also have a shirt that says I love fancy peens.

I shrug as I say, "You're probably right." Then I run off towards my closet to get changed. I grab comfortable clothes that are more appropriate than my current clothing choice. I strip and slip on my clothes as fast as I can.

Putting on a pair of sneakers, I jog out of the room to find Jace already gone. He must be downstairs with the others.

Racing out of my room, I let out a loud squeal of excitement as I run down the stairs. Howe and Alec are at the bottom of the stairs, staring at me wide-eyed. Unfortunately, I'm going too fast to stop, so I launch myself into Howe's arms. He yelps in surprise but catches me.

"Shit, Jane! You scared the hell out of us with your scream. I thought something was wrong." Howe sighs as he holds me closer.

I press my face into his neck and wrap my arms and legs around him. Inhaling deeply, I sigh at his leathery scent. "I'm sorry," I whisper into his neck, "I didn't mean to scare you."

"It's okay, Starlight. We just need this feud with the other gang to end."

Alec comes up behind me and wraps his arms around Howe and me. I hear his deep inhale as he takes in my scent and Howe's. His huff of breath brushes across my neck as he says, "We need to end the threat so we don't freak out every time you scream."

"I didn't even scream; I squealed."

"Sounds the same," Howe and Alec say in unison.

I huff but don't argue. Jace clears his voice from behind us, and I pop my head up. He's got a sad smile as he looks at Howe and Alec holding me tight.

"I'm sorry to interrupt," he says with a sigh. "But we need to leave if we are going to make it to the appointment on time."

Howe growls, and Alec snickers, but they both release me. Setting me softly on my feet, Howe threads his fingers through mine.

I smirk when Alec does the same. Seems that even though they allowed Jace and Zane to cuddle me after my abduction, they weren't as completely unaffected as they pretended to be.

I tighten my fingers in theirs as I smile up at Jace, then flick my gaze to Zane. He's giving me a weary look, so I give him a wide smile. "Let's go get my tattoo!" I drag Howe and Alec behind me as I try to race out the door. Their large bodies slow my progress, but that doesn't stop me.

My pace stopped once I saw Silas and Jax waiting by the armored car. I jump up and down in excitement. "You guys are coming too?!"

Zane walks past, opening the door for me and saying, "Of course, they're coming. We aren't taking any more chances with your safety."

I grin as I release Howe and Alec's hands. It feels really good to have something to smile about again. I approach Zane, stopping once I'm standing and looking up at him. He looks down at me with an arched brow as if expecting me to argue with him as I do with Jace. I normally would to get a rise out of him, but considering recent events, I refrain.

Rising onto the tips of my toes, I press my lips softly against his. I pull away, my lips only a breadth away from his, and say, "Thank you for protecting me."

His light-blue eyes widen at my words before softening. He reaches up, caressing my cheek with the pad of his thumb. "I won't let anyone dim your light again, Sunshine."

I smile as I say, "I love you."

He grunts a response, but I know he's only doing that because people are watching.

I snicker as I weave around him and get into the car. Alec swan dives inside, and I laugh when he lands on my lap. "Get off! You're crushing me," I say with a laugh.

He climbs over my lap and onto the other side, laying his head on my shoulder as he snuggles close.

Howe flies through the door next. He immediately lays his head on my lap, snuggling in close. I smile down at him as I run my fingers through his curly black hair.

Jace sighs when he sees the middle seat is full. He looks into the back seat, then back at us. "Well, this seems unfair."

Howe growls from my lap and says, "You two got her all to yourselves. It's our turn."

Zane puts a hand on Jace's shoulder as he says, "Just get in the car. We're gonna be late."

I smirk as I tease, "Yeah, get in the car, Hades."

He arches a brow. "Are you sassing me, Persephone?"

Howe snickers, and my grin widens. I haven't fucked with Jace in weeks because of everything that has happened, but this feels right. "Maybe I am." I shrug.

Fire sparks in his eyes, and my heart flutters. It's been too long since I've seen the fire in his eyes. His smile turns dark as he climbs into the very back of the vehicle. He settles in the seat so he can lean forward. His lips brush against my ear as he says, "Don't test me, Princess."

A shiver runs down my spine, and Alec snickers on my shoulder. I take a breath to steady my rapidly beating heart before sassing back, "Or what?"

"You'll be punished." He nips my ear before sitting back in his seat.

My blood heats at his words, and my heart pounds. It's been so long since we've played. "Who says I don't want to be punished?" I whisper.

"I heard that, Princess."

I can't stop the smile forming as Silas starts the car, pulling out of the driveway and heading to the tattoo parlor. I'll let him think he won for the moment.

The chime of a bell echoes through the room as we walk through the door. Again, I'm blown away by the space. Silas and Jax lead the way as we pass the front desk. I wave to the young male behind the desk, who waves shyly back. His eyes dart to my guys behind me, and he ducks his head immediately. I snort out a laugh, shaking my head. I suppose my guys can be intimidating when they want to be.

Silas and Jax turn to face outward as they stop in front of a familiar door. I turn the corner expecting to find Blair and Knox, but instead, I'm greeted by two new males. When they turn to look at me, my mouth drops open in shock.

Their eyes widen as well. The smaller one stands up, immediately approaching me and wrapping me in a hug. "What the fuck, girl?! I thought you were fucking dead!"

My voice squeaks as I ask, "Cade?" He had been my main guy when I went to get my piercings. When I started running around all the districts to lose my dad, I lost touch with him.

He pulls away with a wide smile. "Fucking hell, Jelly Bean. I thought your dad got you!"

I wince. He was the only one whom I had told about my dad. Although, it had only been a few months after running away that I decided to change my appearance to better hide from him. "I didn't mean to scare you."

"Jelly Bean?" Jace asks from behind me.

I look over my shoulder with a smile. "It was his nickname for me, so no one knew my name when I went in to get my piercings."

Suddenly, Cade is out of my arms, and a bear of a man is wrapping his arms around me and lifting me off the floor. I squeal with laughter as I wrap my arms around him, hugging him back.

"He's not the only one you worried, JB."

I sigh as I say, "I'm sorry, Tony."

"How the hell do you know Anthony?" Zane asks, confused.

Tony sets me down, and I turn toward my guys, pointing over my shoulder. "Big T was the one who did all of my tattoos before I ran off." I turn back to Cade and Tony, tapping a finger to my lips as I think aloud. "You know . . . now that I think about it, I remember seeing Blair and Knox in passing. But I just pushed them to the background."

I point to Cade and ask, "What are you doing here?"

He smirks as he points to Tony. "I help him set up for these facial tattoos."

"Do a lot of these?" I ask, arching a brow at Tony.

He shakes his head as he points to my guys. "They were the last people I did." He gestures to the seat and says, "Have a seat. I'm all set up." He snaps on a pair of gloves and hands a pair of gloves to Cade as well. Then he hands him a tube of numbing cream.

I sit down in the chair, laying back and getting comfortable. I point to the cream and ask, "Did the guys use numbing cream for theirs?"

Before Cade can answer, a snort sounds behind me. I arch my back to tilt my head to look at my guys. "What?"

Howe points to his face, saying, "They didn't have numbing cream when we got our tattoos."

Settling back into the chair, I shrug. "Then I won't get numbing cream either."

Cade turns to the guys behind me, eyes wide, before looking back down at me. "I would highly recommend using the cream. Without it, your face will feel like it's peeling off by the end of the tattoo."

I shrug again as I close my eyes. "Wouldn't be the first time my face has felt like that."

There's a growl behind me, then Zane's gruff voice echoes throughout the room as he snaps, "Just use the cream, Jane."

"Fuck that shit. I'm a tough-ass bitch. I'm earning my Persephone tattoo."

"What the hell is with your obsession with earning your tattoo?" Jace growls loudly.

I open my eyes to find Tony looking down at me. His eyes search mine before he nods. "We can stop anytime if she needs to." The buzz of the machine starting is loud in the now quiet room.

I close my eyes again as the buzzing gets closer to my face. I am Persephone. I'm the motherfucking Queen of the Underworld.

Chapter Thirty-Six

JANE

I rub healing cream on my face as I look at my reflection in the mirror. The guys gave me a small UV light to use in my bathroom. My face was sore as fuck after getting the tattoo, and it took a good three days for the swelling to go down. It's been a week now, and it's healing amazingly.

Pulling my hand away from my face, I stare at my reflection. I absolutely love my tattoo. One side of my face is identical to Jace's. It's the outline of a skeletal face, while the other side is pure life. I have outlines of flowers, and the outline around my eye looks similar to the sugar skull designs I've seen used for Day of the Dead makeup. Flowers and swirls decorate that side of my face.

Flipping the switch beside me, the room is bathed in light. My hair is now dyed to resemble the difference in my facial tattoo. On the side with the flowers, my hair is still my regular pastel, oil-slick prism. Whereas the side that resembles death is now dark with light-colored highlights. It reminds me of what oil looks like when the light hits it at just the right angle to make small rainbows.

A knock on the door has my gaze flicking up to find Zane. My brows furrow in confusion. He isn't the one who usually comes to collect me. It's usually Howe and Alec, mainly because they love to cause trouble until Jace gets irritated. Or it's Jace, and that's usually because I'm taking too long.

I turn to face Zane as I lean against the counter. "What's wrong?"

He arches a brow as he leans against the door frame. "Does there have to be a problem?"

"You never come and get me before we leave for the cave. So . . . either something is wrong, or you've been body snatched."

He rolls his eyes, but I can see the edge of a smirk. He pushes off the door frame and walks toward me. "There is a small problem, but nothing the Hounds can't handle."

I laugh as I ask, "So there was a problem?" He shrugs as he leans into me, caging me between the counter and his chest. He stares at me momentarily before sighing and settling his forehead against my shoulder. Slowly wrapping my arms around him, I ask, "This isn't a small problem, is it?"

"No," he whispers.

I think of what could possibly be such a big issue, but then I remember. "This is about the gang, isn't it?"

He grunts in answer, and I sigh. At my sigh, he answers, "There have been some issues finding the leader." He pulls me from the counter, wrapping me in a tight hug. "Something bad is going to happen, Sunshine. I can feel it."

I can't exactly tell him everything will be alright because we've had some seriously major shit happen lately. So instead, I wrap him a little tighter and tell him, "We will figure it out together. Somehow, we will make it through. We always do."

He holds me for a few minutes longer before pulling away with a nod. He presses a kiss to my forehead before linking his fingers with mine. "We should probably get downstairs before Jace makes his way up here because we will be late."

I snicker as Zane leads me out of the room. We have to go to the cave for the night for some meetings, but the guys want my face to heal for another week before I am involved in them again. Truthfully, I don't mind. Silas and Jax keep me company while they are in meetings.

Jax jumps out of the passenger seat, and I laugh as he opens the door in a dramatic flourish. He bows at the waist, then looks up with a smirk and winks. I shake my head, smiling. "Thank you, Beta."

He offers his elbow and replies, "Only for you, My Queen."

I take his offered elbow and bump him with my hip, but I continue to play along with his antics. "Thank you so much. I'm ever so grateful for your help, Beta."

He snickers and ushers me into the cave, my guys following. Jace yells from behind us, "Behave! Both of you."

I look at Jax with a wide grin, then yell over my shoulder, "I'm always on my best behavior, Hades."

All of a sudden, I feel a slap on my ass. I let out a squeak and look to my side to find Jace there. Holy shit, he's fast. He gives me a devilish grin as he says, "We all know you are *never* on your best behavior, Persephone."

I shrug but sass back, "That may be true, but we all know you LOVE disciplining me."

Howe howls in laughter as he walks past. "She isn't wrong, Boss."

Jace arches a brow before saying, "Then maybe I should give you a better incentive to behave?"

Leaning forward quickly, I press my lips to his. I pull away just as quickly and revel in the surprise on his face. "Better be off to your meeting, Hades. Wouldn't want to be late," I can't help but add.

He lets out a growl, ready to rip me out of Jax's hold, when Zane grabs him with a smirk. "Let's go, Boss. You can punish her after."

Jace gives me one last lingering look, and I can tell he will spend his time in the meetings coming up with an appropriate punishment for me. A shiver races down my spine at the thought. I give him a wink before Jax leads me away.

He snickers as he leads me to the security room with monitors showing the whole compound. "You love to rile him up, don't you?"

I smile up at Jax as Silas follows behind quietly. "I can't help myself. It's so much fun to see his control shatter."

Silas snorts behind me, and I look over my shoulder to see a smirk on his face. He shakes his head. "Leave it up to you, Seph, to push Hades to the edge."

"Just wait till you find a girl. I'm sure she will do the same," I tease with a smile.

Jax snickers and says, "Alpha here isn't much of a ladies' man."

I smack Jax on the chest. "He doesn't need to be a ladies' man. Mark my words. He will find a feisty-as-fuck girl one day, and if you guys are lucky, she will fall for all of you. Then, she and I will be besties and cause chaos together!"

Jax and Silas look at each other for a moment, then back at me and at the same time say, "I hope the fuck not."

I smirk. "Why not? I need a female bestie. Too much testosterone around here."

Silas sighs as he sits on one of the chairs in front of the screens. "Sit down and watch the screens with us."

Giggling, I do as I'm told and sit between Jax and Silas. I notice Silas bend down before sitting back up. He sets a large coffee in front of me, and I can't stop the grin as I grab it and take a large gulp. Fucking hell, I love this man. "Mmm . . . I love you."

Jax chokes on laughter as Silas' head snaps around to stare at me, eyes wide. "She's talking to the coffee," Jax eventually manages to say.

Silas arches a brow as I shrug. "I do love coffee. But . . . I sorta love you guys too. In a completely brotherly way. I would *not* want to ride your dick."

Silas smacks a hand to his face, and I can see the pink rising on his cheeks. Jax is laughing so hard that he tipped his chair back too far and is now on the ground, howling with laughter.

I can't stop the bubble of laughter that slips through my lips as Silas mutters, "Gods and Goddesses help me if I *ever* find a woman like you."

Jax stands back up, setting his chair straight. He wipes his face as he continues to chuckle, tears streaming from his eyes from laughing so hard. Finally, he sits back on his chair, reaching over to grasp the back of my neck. His smile is so wide as he presses his forehead to mine. "I fucking love you too, Seph."

I grin as he lets go, and I look at the screens surrounding us. On one monitor, I see the meeting chamber where the guys are. The camera is positioned so most of the room is in view. I'm about to look at another monitor when I notice movement. I look back to find that Jace has shifted on his large throne to look right at the camera.

My head tilts, trying to figure out what he's doing. I watch the lights flicker off, and the UV lights fill the room. His skeletal face is now on display, and I see the edges of his tattoo shift. Looking closer, I find that he's smiling at the camera. He presses something on his throne, and his voice suddenly drifts into the room.

"Enjoy your time with the Hounds, My Queen. I'll be coming for you after this meeting is over."

I shiver at his words, and Jax snickers beside me. "It seems you have pushed our boss too far."

I snort a laugh. "It's just so much fun."

Silas huffs another sigh as if he's dealing with rowdy kids. "Let's get back to work. We need to keep an eye on the monitors till the next shift takes over."

I nod and return to watching the screens, Zane's words echoing in my head. If the ache in my stomach is any indication, I also have a bad feeling that something will happen soon.

If only I had known how soon . . .

Chapter Thirty-Seven

Silas

Something is wrong. I stand from my chair, causing Jane to jump in fright.

"What the hell, Alpha?!" She presses a hand to her chest. I look at her briefly before looking back at the screens. Something is off. My eyes jump from screen to screen.

"What is it?" Jax asks, standing from his chair as well. He's staring at the screens frantically, trying to figure out what I'm seeing.

That's the problem, though. It's what I'm *not* seeing. "Where the fuck are our Hounds?"

Jax looks at the screens, his brows furrowing. Then his eyes widen. There it is. He's seeing what I'm seeing now.

Jane stands from her chair and asks, "What's going on?"

Jax's worried eyes meet mine as he answers her question, "There are absolutely no Hounds on any of these screens."

Her brows furrow, "Isn't the point not to be seen?"

"To our enemies? Yes," I say. Fucking hell. "But to the cameras? We should be able to see everyone. These are the eyes of the compound, and we see everyone." My eyes meet hers as I say, "Everyone, Seph."

Her eyes widen as they flick to the screens, landing on her guys in the meeting room. "We can't tell them while they are in the meeting."

"We'll go and make up some bullshit reason the meeting needs to end." Jax grabs his weapons and looks at Jane.

She shakes her head. "You two need to figure out what is going on. You need to find our Hounds." She removes one of the feathered knives from her hair. "I'll head to them and tell them what's going on."

I look down at the daggers she still has sheathed, then back at her with an arched brow. "Why are you using your knives instead of your daggers?"

She smiles at me. "They are small but deadly. I can fight better with these in close combat."

I look at Jax. "You go with her and make sure she gets there safely."

Jax nods, but Jane shakes her head. "No, the two of you need to figure out what is happening. You can cover more ground if there are two of you."

I'm about to argue when she puts a hand on her hip and looks up at me with fire in her eyes. Well, fucking hell. Staring at me intently, she says, "That's an order from your Queen, Alpha. Do you understand?"

My teeth grind as I nod my head. "Yes, My Queen."

She looks to Jax behind her with an arched brow. We exchange glances before he looks back at her with a sigh and nods. "Yes, My Queen."

She smirks as she grabs Jax's hand with her free one. Then, giving it a squeeze, she stands on her tiptoes to brush a kiss on his cheek. "I'll be careful. I promise."

She turns to me, and I stiffen. I have no idea how to deal with this woman, but I find that I can't help but feel attached to her. She's the first person to poke and poke at me till I had no choice but to accept her. She's the little sister I didn't know I wanted. Huffing out a sigh, I open my arms. I know she wants a hug, and I find it hard to deny her.

A smile touches her lips as she wraps her free arm around me and squeezes. She releases me, pressing a soft kiss to my cheek as well. I feel the crack in my chest. The barrier I've held around myself for so long seems to crumble the more time I spend around her. She looks up at me with a soft smile and says, "Be careful, big guy."

I snort a laugh and press a soft kiss on her forehead. "Be careful yourself, Seph."

She steps away from both of us, taking a deep breath before leaving the safety of our watch. Jax slaps his hand down on my shoulder as we watch her leave. "Didn't think we would ever bring someone into our little family again after Greyson died," he whispers.

My chest burns with the familiar pain of losing my older brother. I had to step up and become the big brother after that. I have to admit, the job wasn't as easy as he made it look. But I don't regret a single moment with my brothers. I love them. I don't say it much, but I do. Rubbing the pain in my chest, I say, "She snuck her way in."

He snorts a laugh. "She sure the fuck did, Brother."

Jane

I take off down the hallway, running toward the meeting room. Jax and Silas were right, though. I haven't seen a single Hound on my way here. Usually, I see at least five or six on my way through these halls. I also haven't encountered a single reason why the Hounds wouldn't be in their spots. The sickening feeling in my stomach from earlier grows heavier. Something terrible is going to happen tonight. Again.

I skid to a stop in front of the door to the meeting when it swings open. Jace stands there, eyes wide, as he sees me standing there, out of breath.

I probably shouldn't have run all the way here, and holy shit, I'm out of shape. I hold up a finger when I see him about to ask a question. "Give me a sec," I pant. As I try to get my breathing under control, I watch the others come up behind Jace. Good, that saves me the trouble of finding them.

"Are you good, Princess?"

Taking a deep breath, I nod. "Okay, so there's a problem. Silas, Jax, and I haven't seen a single Hound on any of the cameras. So they went to figure out what's going on. I told them I would notify you guys of what's happening."

Jace arches a brow and asks, "They left you alone?"

Bristling at his words, I put a hand on my hip. "Excuse me. I *am* the Queen of the Underworld, am I not?"

Jace's eyes narrow. "That is not what I meant."

"Then what did you mean, my King?"

Fire sparks in his eyes at my words. He steps into the hallway so we are only a breath away from each other and says, "I only meant to assure that my Queen was properly protected, considering we may have intruders."

I stand a bit taller and ask, "Do you not believe me capable of defending myself?"

He stares at me for a moment and sighs. Then, he caresses my cheek with his thumb before tilting his head and pressing his lips softly to mine. He pulls away enough to look into my eyes, and I notice his dark brown eyes seem even darker now. They are filled with too many emotions for me to narrow down what he's feeling right now. "I do not have the heart or will to live without you, My Queen. I have almost lost you too many times for my liking already. The more people guarding you, the better," he whispers the words across my lips like a soft caress.

All my anger seems to sizzle out of me. He's right; I can't lose them again, either. I sigh as I reach up to cup the side of his face. He nuzzles into my hand and closes his eyes, his body shuddering at my touch. "I would not have left their safety if I didn't think I could handle myself. I promise I will not leave your side from this moment on."

He turns to kiss the palm of my hand before looking at me, nodding before pulling away. He stands close but doesn't take my hand, allowing me to reach for my weapons if needed. "Seems we have an intruder."

Zane stands in the doorway and says, "We should investigate outside and find out where our Hounds have disappeared to. Seph should have been able to see them on the cameras."

Jace nods before looking at me. "Ready for battle, My Love?"

I remove my daggers from their sheaths with a dark smile. "I do love some evening bloodshed."

Jace smirks as he nods for us to move down the hallway toward the front doors. Howe snorts a laugh behind me, and I look over my shoulder to see him grinning. "Seems our Queen is bloodthirsty this evening."

Walking down the hallway, I take in my newest outfit. I'm wearing leathers meant for battle. I was drawn to them this morning . . . now I know why. "I do not like when people believe us weak and press upon our territory."

Alec's voice echoes as he says, "I love when you go all Persephone on us. Fucking sexy."

I grin as we continue down the hallway. The enemy will pay if they have harmed my Hounds. I am the Queen of the Underworld, and it is about damn time people understand that.

Jace slams through the front doors, and we follow behind, slipping into formation. I wasn't prepared for the utter silence that greeted us. There are no Hounds. Anywhere. The doors behind us shut, then there's a click. What the fuck? I turn to find Alec trying to rip the doors open, but nothing happens. Our doors should not lock on their own. The only people controlling anything in this compound are in the security room.

Fucking hell . . . someone must have hacked into our system. The only way anyone could hack into the system is from the inside. No one could get through Howe's protections . . . except if they had access from the inside. Which means we have another snake in our cave. Son of a bitch!

I look over to Howe to find his eyes glowing with rage. Someone on the security team betrayed us.

I hear the scuff of boots and look around to find we are no longer alone.
Fuck . . . Guess we found the gang that is trying to take control. We've found
the leader. Men pour out of the fog around us, and the guys shift closer to
me. Fuck. FUCK. FUCK!

We are surrounded. No security. No Hounds. Just us.

FUCK . . .

Chapter Thirty-Eight

JANE

A lone figure walks out between the crowd of people surrounding us. The man is wearing a Persian mask; at least, I think it's a Persian mask. I remember briefly that the Persians were enemies of the Greeks, which makes this whole situation ironic but also highly irritating.

His voice sounds distorted as he says, "Seems the rulers of the Underworld are about to fall."

"Says who?" Jace snarls.

The man gestures to the people behind him. I'm not sure how many people are followers versus people he conned into working with him. Although, at the moment, that doesn't matter. He has the numbers.

We weren't expecting an ambush from the gang we had been trying to track down for weeks. We should have been notified that they were out here, but that would be hard, considering no one was out here to notify us. I look around, hoping to see any of our Hellhounds. They should be here by now. Which means something is very wrong. Silas and Jax should have been here by now as well.

The gang leader takes a step forward, moving closer to us. His crooked smile shining through the mask. "Are you looking for your Hellhounds?"

Jace sneers. "What the fuck do you mean?"

He points to me, then to Jace. "I can see it in your eyes. You're wondering where your backup is." The guys behind him snicker as he continues,

"We've created a bit of a . . ." He uses the tip of his gun to make a swirling motion in the air. "Diversion."

He waves a few of his men forward, and we all instantly crouch down in a fighting position. I feel Howe at my back instantly as he takes my six. Zane does the same to Jace. Alec takes the spot right next to me. I huff a sigh. Fucking hell. Here's to hoping Tony did a great job creating our weapons.

The guys had let it slip that Tony had made my new daggers. He had also made Zane a scythe, and I have to admit, I'd never seen that man smile as big as I did that day. For Howe, Tony had made custom double daggers attached with a chain so he could throw and swing them around. What makes them even better is that the blades look like the bottom jaw of a Canine. The sharp points look like canine teeth. Tony had given Alec a sharp as fuck spear, but he left it inside the compound. At the moment, I was glad he had several guns strapped to him. Jace also was given a weapon, but I haven't gotten the chance to see it. He also has several guns and knives strapped to him.

The gang boss laughs as he gestures to his goons. "Play fair, boys. Don't kill them too fast."

The men close in to begin their fun. I begin slicing. I fight off as many as I can without breaking our huddle. But there are too many of them, and I'm slammed to the ground. Jumping back up as fast as I can, I find the others now feet away from me instead of inches. The men try to push us even further apart from each other as we fight off multiple assailants.

My breaths are coming quickly as I fight with everything inside to cut down the men attacking me. It's as if they are a hydra. Once I cut down one, another takes his place. I can hear the grunts and yells of my men around me. No longer able to see me, or I them. I'm suddenly pushed onto the ground, and a body slams down on top of me, holding me down. I scream in frustration as my daggers are ripped out of my hands, and a boot slams down on my head, smashing my face into the dirt.

"Oh, let the Queen up enough to see her men." the gang leader says with a laugh.

The body on top of me shifts so he can pull my arms around my back. He pulls them high, and I have to hold back my groan of pain. The boot on my head lifts, and I'm about to fight until I feel cold metal press against my head. Fucking hell.

Growls from my guys echo around me, and I try to peek through the curtain of my hair. Well, those fucking hair ties were shit. My stomach drops at what I see. All of my guys are being restrained, granted it's by several men. But . . . restrained nonetheless, and they won't do anything with a gun to my head.

My eyes narrow when I hear the gang leader laugh. "Seems the demons of the Underworld can be tamed after all. All I needed to do was take their Queen."

I grunt and snarl, "Who the fuck says you have the fucking Queen?"

The leader looks in my direction, then snaps his fingers. The metal kissing my head is removed, but I scream when I'm pulled up by my hair. I gnash my teeth and growl, trying to fight until the bite of metal is against my temple.

The leader smirks at me and continues his evil monologue, "As I was saying. If I want to take over the Underworld, I need to take the Queen." His eyes shift from me to Jace. "But we all know that although the Queen may hold the power of the Demons, the King holds all the power of the Underworld. So if I want the Underworld, I need to take both."

He points his gun at Jace for a second before sighing. "But this seems so very anticlimactic so . . ." He points to the guy standing beside Jace and the guy holding him. "Let's see what happens when he slices his throat open."

Then, there's a knife to Jace's throat, and I see him flinch as it presses hard into his skin. I start fighting against my restraints, as do my other guys.

The leader laughs with glee and says, "There we go! So much fight! That's what I wanted."

A click sounds next to my ear, and I instantly stop fighting. This fucker just pulled the hammer back. My guys immediately look in my direction. Their eyes are wide at realizing just how bad our situation is. The leader starts to pace in front of us.

He smiles. "So, who should go first? Your Queen? Or your King?"

My eyes meet Jace's, and he gives me a sad smile as he whispers, "I will see you soon, My Queen."

I shake my head frantically. Fuck that! Fuck this shit. "No! You are not fucking leaving us. You fight! You fight till the end!"

Jace's eyes flare with anger. "There's a gun to your fucking head and a knife to my throat! What would you have me do, Persephone?!"

I don't know! I . . . I don't know. I look at my other men. Howe is growling like an animal but doesn't try to fight. He won't with a gun ready to shoot me dead. Next, my gaze shifts to Alec. He's looking at me with a sad smile. "It will be okay, Seph," he whispers.

My eyes burn as they shift to my last man. "Zane," my voice breaks on his name.

I can see the war in his eyes. The need to protect. He can't, though. He's incapable of protecting his family, and it's killing him. His voice sounds gruff as he says, "If we fall into the depths of the Underworld, may we fall together."

My vision blurs as my eyes meet Jace's once more. With a sad smile still on his face, he says, "May our souls be reunited in the Meadows of Asphodel. And if the Gods and Goddesses find us worthy, may we enter the Elysian Fields."

I choke on a sob as I watch the knife dig deeper into his skin. I begin to thrash against the men holding me, not caring about the gun to my head.

I scream against their hold as I pray to anyone who can hear me. Someone fucking help us!

As if the Gods and Goddesses themselves answered my prayer, the man holding a knife to Jace's throat explodes in a spray of red. My eyes widen as I watch an arrow shoot right through his head. Holy fucking shit!

Before anyone can even react, another arrow shoots through the neck of the man restraining Jace. He stands quickly with a smile that I have to admit would make me pee myself in fright if it were directed at me.

Then suddenly, several arrows follow the first two, taking down the men holding Howe, Alec, Zane, and me. I look around, trying to figure out where the fuck the arrows are coming from. What the fuck am I doing? A sane person would drop to the floor, ensuring they didn't get hit.

I look around in the darkness and see dark figures emerging from behind the curve of the cave. My eyes widen when I see it's Blair and her guys. WHAT. THE. FUCK.

"Nice of you to show up, Arty," Howe says with a grunt as he stands from the ground brushing off the dirt.

"Am I not usually late to the party, Cerby?" She snickers as she makes her way over to us, bow in hand, currently aimed at the gang leader.

Jace laughs roughly and says, "I was hoping you would show up, Artemis."

She just shrugs as her guys fan out beside her. "You know how these three are."

Knox snorts and replies, "You should know by now I can never pick just one weapon."

Blair rolls her eyes. "Yes, well, you should know by now which are your favorites, so just pick those."

He shrugs. "I'm the God of War; what do you expect?"

She huffs out a sigh as if this is an argument they regularly have. "Just pick a fucking weapon, Ares! It isn't that fucking hard!"

Cade walks in between the two and claps his hands together. "Okay, you two get it together. We have bad guys to fight."

Tony finally speaks up, "I agree with Theseus."

Cade smiles up at Tony. "Thanks, Hephaestus."

Tony grunts as he looks over at me. Then, arching a brow, he asks, "You good, Persephone?"

I shake off my surprise and nod. "Um . . . I think so." What the fuck just happened?

Chapter Thirty-Nine

JANE

Trying to get a handle on the situation, I point toward Blair and ask, "Were you the one who shot those arrows?"

She smiles, still keeping her bow pointed at the leader, ready to shoot if he moves. "I would love to say those were all mine, but Apollo also came to help. Seems he got the 911 call from Alpha."

Apollo? Who the fuck is Apollo, and why don't I know who everyone is? I'm about to ask just that when a man walks around the corner of the cave. My jaw drops. Luka?! But he looks different in his dark leather outfit and bright, golden contacts. Where the fuck did he get contacts like that? Wait . . . back on subject. He's carrying a bow and has an arrow ready to sheathe if needed.

He smirks as he lifts his bow in greeting. "Evening. Seems like a nice night for bloodshed."

I can't help but snort. "Apollo, really?"

He shrugs, continuing his way over to us. "I have a bright personality."

I laugh again. "A bright personality . . . right. And It has nothing to do with the fact that he associates with wolves?"

He smirks, saying, "That may have a little to do with it too."

Remembering that enemies still surround us, I look around. Unfortunately, though, I have to admit that their numbers have plummeted. Seems some of his followers didn't want to stick around when they found out Hades had backup. Deadly backup.

The leader sneers. "You still don't have your Hounds, and you're outnumbered."

Luka points at him with the arrow in his hand as he says, "I wouldn't get too arrogant. You currently have an arrow pointed at your head. Also, the Hound thing won't be an issue much longer."

Jace's smile darkens as his eyes narrow on the leader. "Is that so, Apollo?"

Luka nods. "Just got a text from Alpha. It seems some of the cave walls were destroyed, and the Hounds got trapped. The debris has been moved, and they are on their way back."

Just as Luka finishes, Silas and Jax exit through the front doors of the cave. Weren't those locked? I watch as the door Silas pushes through seems to close unevenly behind them. Seems he was too pissed to mind that it was locked.

Zane looks over at them and yells, "Where are the Hounds?"

Silas growls as he answers, "They are securing our compound again." He doesn't stop marching over to us until he stands before the gang leader. With a sneer, he snaps his fist out, landing a hit right to the guy's face. The leader falls to the ground, ripping off his broken mask. He's holding his now bleeding nose as blood streams down his face. Silas looks over to Jace and apologizes, "Sorry, Hades. I needed to do that."

Jace snorts a laugh. "I'll let it slide, Alpha."

Silas looks back down at the leader and snarls, "That was for my Hounds." He takes a deep breath before looking over to find Luka. I see the slight tilt of his lips as he gives him a nod.

"Did you get that out of your system, Alpha?" Blair questions with a smirk.

I turn toward the leader when I notice him move. The gun he'd been holding slipped out of his hand when Silas punched him, but he's reaching for it now. Then suddenly, a flaming arrow slices across my vision and pierces the top of his hand. He screams as the flames sizzle out.

Holy fucking shit, that was cool. How did she get the arrow to burst into flame like that? That was some major Katniss Everdeen shit, and I am here for it. How can I get my hands on some flaming arrows like that? Could I get ones that blow shit up too? I'm pulled out of my inner ramblings when I hear a snort of laughter.

"Did you think my arrows were just for show? Yes, the men were talking, but don't think for a moment that I forgot about you. My arrow was pointed at you for a reason." Blair nocks another arrow, aiming at him again. She gives him a sinister as she asks, "Would you like to test me again, Fucker?"

A giggle slips out between my lips. Everyone except Blair looks at me with raised eyebrows. I shrug. "What? That was funny."

Jace smirks as Zane facepalms. I can see the smile he's trying to hide, though. Howe and Alec come up to stand beside me. Howe bumps my shoulder with a grin and asks, "What part was funny? The bloodshed part or Arty pointing out that she was the badass of the group?"

"Is," Arty corrects from her position.

Howe rolls his eyes. "Is, whatever."

"If you're going to point out my badassery, make sure you do it correctly."

I smirk as he narrows his eyes at her, and I bump his shoulder to get his attention back on me. "Both," I say with a wink. He bursts out laughing.

Alec snickers and says, "Our Queen loves some bloodshed."

Jace chuckles. "Alright, My Queen, where shall we take our prisoner?"

Looking around us once more, I notice that there are no longer any followers encircling us. It seems they ran when they had the chance, and I don't foresee them going up against us again soon, considering their leader is currently bleeding out on the ground. I huff a sigh and tap a finger to my lips in thought. As I walk closer to the leader, I consider what to do with him. Then I notice the arrow still sticking out of his hand.

Reaching down quickly, I snatch the feathers of the arrow and pull. He immediately follows the action with a scream of pain. He snarls as he reaches out with his other hand. I'm not sure what he planned on doing because his actions pause when the gun barrel rests against his skull.

I smirk when I see that it's Jace. He growls as he says, "I would advise you to think hard about your next actions, or your skull will be decorating the ground."

I shiver at his words, my smirk turning into a wide grin as I look down at the leader. "It would be a shame to get brain matter all over my new clothes. I'm not a fan of wearing skull and brain matter. Much too messy for my liking. Plus, blood is a bitch to get out."

"You're wearing black, Seph," Tony points out.

I shrug as I smirk. "Doesn't make it any easier to get the blood out," I mutter.

Cade speaks up next. "But no one would know because it's black."

"Maybe, but *I* would know blood was ruining my outfit."

Zane sighs. "I would just buy you a new outfit. Can we move on to what to do with this utter waste of time? I want to get on with my evening."

Jace nods. "Yes, I would also like to get back to my evening. I believe you and I had plans, Princess."

I arch a brow, trying to remember what he's talking about. He smirks, then I remember the car ride here. Fuck . . . I am in trouble. My body flushes, thinking about the possible punishments I could get tonight.

"Is he talking about sex?" Knox asks in a not-so-hushed voice. My cheeks blaze red at his question. Then, hearing a thump, I look over and find Knox holding his head while Tony shakes his in disappointment.

I see Blair's smirk when she says, "Thank you, Hephaestus."

"A pleasure, Artemis," Tony grunts.

Shaking myself, I look over at Silas. "Could you take him to the room my father was in?"

Understanding fills his gaze, and he nods, saying, "Yes, my Queen. Would you like me to give him a dose? I can fill the room too."

I look back down to the leader who caused us so much trouble over the last few months. I smile at him and reply, "Both will do, Alpha."

He nods, looking toward his brothers. "Help me get this fucker down to the dungeons."

Jax gives me a devilish grin as he walks toward us. He looks down at the leader and asks, "Permission to have some fun, Seph?"

I snort out a laugh but give him a nod. "Permission granted, Beta."

He rubs his hands together in glee, then looks toward his younger brother and says, "Let's get him down there, Apollo. I can't wait to have my fun."

Luka huffs out a sigh, shaking his head with a smirk. "I'm glad I don't have to deal with this shit on a daily basis." He reaches down, grabbing the male's arm while Jax grabs his other arm. They escort him back to the cave.

"I'll follow behind to make sure he doesn't cause any trouble," Blair says before giving us a nod and following the others. Her males circle her as they trail behind. I watch until they are out of sight.

I huff out a sigh of my own, I turn to my guys. Shit, this has turned into a long night. I look between my guys before asking, "What now?"

Jace smiles darkly. "Now, the demons come out to play."

I arch a brow, then Jace and Zane rush toward me. My eyes widen as Alec and Howe jump out of the way. I squeal as I turn to run toward the cave, almost making it to the door before I'm lifted, flipped, and thrown over a shoulder. Lifting my head, I find Jace being tackled to the ground by Howe and Alec.

A hand slaps down on my ass as I'm hustled into the cave. "You're mine," Zane says with a growl.

I laugh as he makes his way to our bedrooms. "You do realize that he will fight through Howe and Alec to find us?"

Zane chuckles darkly. "I'll already be fucking you by then."

Chapter Forty

JANE

I screech when I'm thrown onto a bed. Searching around, I realize I'm in Zane's room. I peer up to find his ice-blue eyes looking down at me. He may not be able to see me out of his left eye, but that doesn't make his stare any less penetrating. "We are covered in dirt and blood. Shouldn't we take a shower first?"

In an instant, he rips his shirt over his head and pulls down his pants. The large bulge in his tight boxer briefs draws my eyes down before I shoot them back up to meet his. "Strip," he orders with a growl.

I feel a rush between my legs, and know I'm instantly wet for this man. Biting my lower lip, I do as I'm told. Stripping off my blood and dirt-covered clothes, I'm in only my bra and underwear when he pounces.

His lips meet mine in a hurried frenzy as he pulls and tugs at my bra. Finally finding the clasp, he unhooks it. He throws it, not once removing his lips from mine. He massages my breasts in his large hands, and I groan into his mouth.

He pulls away, panting as he looks down at me. "I fucking need you, Sunshine. I need you like I need my next breath. You're the only one who can chase away the darkness."

I lift enough to press my lips lightly to his, then pull away just enough so that my words whisper across his lips. "The light only shines bright in the darkness. I love every bit of your darkness. I love you, Zane."

He groans as he jumps off the bed, ripping off his boxers. Jumping back onto the bed, he rips my underwear off, throwing it behind him. Positioning himself so that he's hovering over me, he rubs his cock across my clit, and I moan.

Lowering so our lips are only a breadth apart, he says, "I fucking love you so much, Sunshine." He then slams into me and smashes his lips to mine to quiet my scream at the sudden fullness. His movements turn frenzied as he devours my mouth. I moan into his mouth as I wrap my arms around his neck, pulling him closer. I do the same with my legs, making him hit deeper each time.

With his fingers tangled in my hair, he pulls away just far enough to look into my eyes as he pants. He hits the perfect spot on his next thrust, and I scream in ecstasy as my cunt squeezes his cock. But he doesn't stop his movements. No, it seems only to make his thrusting more frantic.

I open my eyes, not realizing I had closed them, to find his ice-blue eyes staring back at me. Some of his hair is coming out of his bun, cascading around his face. His eyes bore into mine, and I see his need. The need for control and to make sure I'm safe after failing to protect his family.

I move my hands to tangle my fingers in his hair. Removing the tie holding his hair up allows the long dark-brown locks to curtain around us. The red tips seem to glow in the lantern light. I tighten my fingers against the hair at his skull. "I'm here. I'm safe. You protected your Sunshine."

His growl sounds like a whine as he presses his lips against mine again. Surprisingly soft this time. I feel one of his hands release its hold on my hair, then snake its way between us. Then I feel his thumb press down on my clit. My fingers tighten in his hair as I moan.

Pulling away, he whispers, "Come for me, Sunshine." He rubs then presses on my clit as he slams into me, hitting that spot just right, making me explode. Zane grunts as he follows, and my cunt squeezes his cock hard.

He continues a slow rhythm of thrusts until the pleasure dwindles to a low hum.

He presses his forehead against mine, his cock still inside me. Making me feel full but satisfied. A throat clearing has my eyes widening. Zane laughs softly above me, lifting to look into my eyes. He smirks as he says, "I told you I would be fucking you by the time he found us. Seems I overestimated his ability to get away from the others. Thought we would be mid-fuck when he found us."

Jace growls from the doorway. "You fucking asshole."

Zane chuckles again as he flips us without issue. I'm now on top, straddling him as he lies beneath me. He winks up at me, and I can't stop the smile that spreads across my face. He's feeling playful, and I'm certainly not going to stop having fun if that's what he wants.

Peering over my shoulder, I see Jace still standing in the doorway like a dark cloud. I smirk at him as I taunt, "Are you going to come have fun with us, or are you just going to stand there like a pervy perv watching from the doorway?"

He arches a brow. "Pervy perv?"

I shrug. "If the shoe fits."

"Is that so, Princess?" He makes his way over to us, slowly stripping as he does. By the time he gets to the bed, he's wearing only his black boxer briefs. Hum ... seems I got boxer brief boys.

My eyes drop to his covered dick, and I grin as I look back up at him. "It is so. So are you going to have fun with us, or are you going to let that large dick go to waste?"

Jace smirks as he comes up behind me and then presses on my back until I'm lying on Zane with my chest pressed against his. "So you want to play, Princess?"

My breaths are coming quickly, and I can't stop the words from sounding breathy as I say, "Yes."

I can hear the smile in his voice as he replies, "Very well, Princess." Then his hand comes down and smacks my ass. Hard.

I squeal at the sudden pain, but it quickly becomes a moan of pleasure because Zane's cock is still inside me.

Zane groans as his hands come up to settle on my thighs. "Fucking hell, she loved that brother. Her pussy fucking fluttered around my cock." I notice that Zane's breathing is changing too, but he remains still, refusing to thrust his hips.

Jace slaps my ass again, and Zane groans. Fucking hell! Should getting spanked feel this good and turn me on this much? Jace's hand softly brushes across my ass after each slap.

He growls as he says, "I expect you to come around his cock. You will soak his cock from me only slapping your ass, do you understand?"

"Can he fuck me as you do it?"

"No. You only get the satisfaction of his cock inside you."

I whine, "That doesn't seem fair!"

His hand brushes across my ass again as he says, "This is your punishment. Now do you understand, Princess? I can rip you off his cock right now, and then you don't get anything."

"No!" I screech.

Jace chuckles as he says, "Then take your punishment like a good girl, Princess."

"Fine," I growl.

He slaps my ass hard again. "Excuse me?"

I pant and say, "I'll take my punishment like a good girl."

Rubbing my ass again, he says, "Very good. Now take your punishment." He slaps my ass again, one after another, not allowing me to take a breath between slaps. "Don't you fucking come until I say you can," he orders in a low growl.

I'm a fucking mess. Tears are streaming down my face with how badly I need to come. This is too much. Too fucking much!

"Brother, let her come," Zane pants below me. "She's got a fucking death hold on my cock."

Jace hums at Zane's words. "Very well. You will come on this next strike, do you understand, Princess?"

"Yes! Yes . . . please," I whimper.

When Jace's hand meets my ass again, I bite Zane's chest. Hard. He grunts, squeezing my thighs hard as he comes as well. Zane whispers, "Fucking hell."

Jace chuckles behind us as I feel his fingers slip between my legs to where Zane and I are joined. "Such a good girl. You soaked his cock just like I told you to."

I feel him collecting our combined release, then his fingers slip between my ass cheeks, and I whimper. "Do you want me here, Princess?"

I nod frantically. He continues to circle the hole. "I need your words, Princess."

"Yes," I whimper.

Jace groans as he inserts his thumb into my ass. I whimper a bit at the new feeling. Zane immediately grabs my face, pressing his lips to mine, distracting me from the foreign feeling. Then Jace changes it up by pressing two fingers into my ass, prepping me to take his cock. To be honest, I'm not sure how I will handle his cock, considering the piercings he has, but I'm willing to try.

"Bro, pull out for a second so I can lube myself up," Jace says as he pulls his fingers out of my ass. I whine at the sudden absence, and Jace chuckles as my whine deepens when Zane pulls out of my cunt, and Jace slips in. He thrusts a few times before pulling all the way out, which makes me growl.

He slaps my ass softly. "Stop growling. We will be fucking you into mindless delirium in a moment."

Zane slips back into position, and I moan as his cock slips back into my needy cunt. "You're not going to freak out if our dicks touch, are you?" Zane asks.

Jace grunts as he says, "My dick is hard as a rock, and I'm about to fuck our woman's ass. Do you really think I have a problem with our dicks touching?"

"Fucking fuck me already," I screech.

Jace spreads my ass cheeks and presses the head of his cock at my rear entrance. Pressing in as he says, "As my Queen wishes." He takes it slow as he presses further into me. I whimper at the feel of each piercing as he enters. When he's fully seated in my ass, he waits, panting.

I figured I would need more time, but truthfully I just wanted them to fuck me already. "I'm ready."

Jace remains still as Zane begins moving under me. He groans as his dick rubs up against Jace's. I know he can feel Jace's piercings through the thin wall.

I hear Jace pant behind me as he forces himself to stay still. His fingers on my hips tighten as he says, "Fucking hell! Dude, is this supposed to feel this good?"

Zane huffs out a laugh as he continues thrusting into me from below. "What, my dick sliding against yours as I fuck our woman's cunt, and your dick fills her ass?"

I groan. "Do you guys need a minute? Do I need to get Howe and Alec, or can you guys actually fuck me? You promised me bliss. I'm getting a little jealous of this bromance going on."

Zane snorts a laugh before slamming into me hard, causing Jace and me to moan. "Then bliss you shall get." Jace's fingers slip between my thighs to play with my clit as Zane massages and pinches my nipples.

The overwhelming feeling of being full with two of my boys makes my body vibrate with need. Zane slams into me, hitting just the right spot to make me see spots before my body explodes in pleasure. They both moan as my body clamps down on them. It doesn't take much longer for them to follow me into bliss.

We sit there for a moment, trying to catch our breath, when I hear clapping behind us. I thump my head against Zane's chest as he chuckles. Jace slowly pulls out and covers me with a sheet. He falls beside us on the bed as I slide off of Zane and drop to his other side.

Looking to the door, I find a smiling Alec while Howe stands there with a grin and claps. "Bravo! That was an amazing show. Wish we had been invited."

I snicker as I pat the bed beside me. "We can have some more fun in a moment. I just need some rest." Then, I look down at myself and realize I'm still covered in dirt and blood. With a grimace, I say, "I should probably take a shower."

Zane drops an arm over my abdomen to stop me from getting up. "The sheets can be changed. Just enjoy the moment for a bit. We have time."

Howe jumps onto the bed and says, "All the time in the world."

Alec comes over and sits beside me. He slides his fingers into my hair, giving my scalp a massage. "What do you want to do now, Moonbeam?"

I look between all my guys before answering. "Be with you."

Alec smiles as Howe moves to hover over me. I giggle as he gives me a quick kiss on the lips. He grins down at me and says, "You already have us, Starlight."

Zane speaks up beside me, "What do you want to do?"

I think about it for a moment before grinning wide. "Rule the world, of course."

Jace laughs as he sits up to look over at me. His eyes are filled with laughter as he says, "That can be arranged, Princess."

Epilogue

JACE

I can't stop the grin from spreading across my face as I watch Jane have fun with our new prisoner. We have been working over the gang leader who tried to take over our territory. We've managed to get the names of all the politicians who paid him to cause us issues. I've already contacted my Hounds, who are undercover nationwide. They have the politicians handled. Right now, we are just having some fun with the man.

Watching Jane take control is sexy as fuck. Seeing her now in her full Persephone persona torturing this man has me hard as fuck. I shift to rearrange the large bulge in my pants.

Zane catches the movement and looks at me, smirking when he sees me adjusting myself. I arch a brow, daring him to say something. He chuckles and looks away, continuing to watch our woman. I sigh as I watch him. He's just as gone with our girl as I am, but I've never seen him as happy as he is right now. She may be his Sunshine, but I've never seen my brother shine as much as he does when he's with her.

My attention is brought back to Jane when I hear the man scream. I watch as she skips over to the table with all of our knives and other torture instruments. Noticing a knife sticking out of the man's thigh, I shake my head with a smirk. I thought we were dark and sinister fuckers, but our woman can be just as dark.

Shifting my gaze to her, I see her hand hovering over the tools. She's humming to herself as she swings her hips to whatever song is playing in her head. I notice her hands are covered in blood as she swipes up a rod with a sharp point at the end. It's not very big, maybe the size of a pencil. She looks at it for a moment before turning around.

She grins at me and asks, "Do you think I could shove this up his dick?"

I choke on my saliva, and Zane howls with laughter. She looks back down at the rod, then back up at me. Her face turns sour, and she says, "Nevermind. That would require me to touch his dick."

I huff out a breath as I pinch the bridge of my nose—this woman. I look back up at her, giving her a stern look as I say, "How about we let Alpha and Beta have some fun now? We have meetings to get to."

She sighs before throwing the rod over her shoulder and whining, "I hate meetings."

Zane takes her bloody hand in his and reminds her, "You wanted to take over the world, did you not?"

She groans but nods and walks over to me. Sliding her other bloody hand into mine, she says. "Let's go take over the world then."

I smile, and we leave the room, but not before the man behind us lets out an ear-splitting scream. I did promise this woman the world.

She's our Queen. Our Goddess. Our Persephone. We created this world for her. We are her demons to rule and use. We are the rulers of the Underworld.

About the Author

Ivy Cole is a longtime lover of writing and has wanted to publish her books for years. She loves Reverse Harem of many kinds. She's an indie author and can't wait to share future books with you.

Want to follow Ivy Cole and see future books? Follow her at:

https://www.facebook.com/groups/508646927449550/

Want all things, Ivy Cole? Click her Linktree to access all her social media accounts.

https://linktr.ee/ivycoleauthor

Also By

<u>Books Also by Ivy Cole</u>

Underground Syndicate Series:

Underworld

Tartarus

Why Choose Fables:

Meddling with Madness (Wonderland Retelling)

The Washington Wraiths

Ice Me Baby (Liz, Mac, Dean)